i

c

o

p

e

For more information, find CCM at:

http://copingmechanisms.net

THE IN-

MATTHEW

BETWEENS

SIMMONS

For Abby & Ash & Alice Blue.

"We are all deep in a hell each moment of which is a miracle."
—**E.M. Cioran**

"I stood there shivering in my pajamas and watched the whole world go up in flames. And when it was all over I said to myself, 'Is that all there is to a fire?'"
—**Peggy Lee**

The End, Temporarily
This Mountain I Built
Apple
Defenestration: A Love Story
Grackles
Sleep Underground
Teenage Motorcycle and Love Tragedy Story
The Longer You Wait Before You Look Through the
Glass, The Farther Away the Ships Will Be
Styles
Baka Is the Night
3 Ways I Don't Want to Die
Underlings: A Rebuke
Americans After America
The In-Betweens
Ishpeming

We Got Lost Along the Way, a novelette
Up North, a novella

THE END, TEMPORARILY

A man made a pact with God. "End me temporarily," he said, "and allow everyone else that has been ended to return."

"What?" said God.

"End me. No Heaven. No Hell. No Limbo. No nothing. No me. Me nothing. Make me nothing for a temporary period of time, and bring everyone else you have ended back, so that everyone who has not ended can spend time with everyone who has. But bring me back eventually. And then, do whatever you will with the ones who you have ended. And brought back. Because of our deal."

"This is complicated," said God.

"But you get me, right?"

"I'm God. Of course I get you. I didn't mean it was complicated for me. Nothing is complicated for me."

"Everything is complicated for me," said the man.

"As it should be," said God.

"Welcome to my world," said the man.

"No. It's my world," said God. "Welcome to my world."

"Not as nice as I thought it would be," said the man.

"I could end you," said God.

"This is a part of the deal I was proposing."

"So it is."

11

"Well?" said the man.

Blink went the man.

Blink went the man. He was back.

"What happened?" said the man.

"My father came back," said an elderly gentleman. "He said everything went gone and then suddenly, there he was."

"My mother, she also came back," said a person of maybe 30 years of age. "And she reported something similar, although, first she said she saw a tunnel. A nice, long tunnel."

"My sister came back and said that she had spent what seemed to her to be a million million years playing fetch with our old dog. She said that even though she was playing fetch for a million million years, she was never once bored. And neither was the dog."

"I have a living, real, breathing dog now," said a man who felt it was okay to interrupt, "and I can tell you that it is on Earth as it is in Heaven. My living, real, breathing, drooling, panting, tail-wagging dog can play fetch for a million million years and never once get anything like anywhere near tired. Love that dog."

"Love that dog, too," said the woman with the sister.

"Love that mother," said the woman with the mother.

"Love my daddy and wish he would come back some more."

And the man made another call to God. "Okay, God. Seemed like that whole thing went over well. Tell you what. You can go ahead and end me again—temporarily. And if I allow you to do so, I want you to bring back all the other people you ended. And I want everyone to have some real, wholesome quality time with their families. And then bring me back and make them go away again, if that's what you want. The making them go away, I mean. I mean, make me come back. Always, me coming back. Them going away is your pick. You pick. As long as I get to come back. I mean, I'm making this sacrifice. I don't get to see all the people who you made go away who I want to see. So, fair deal. I should get to go away—totally and completely go away—and then also get to come back. A fair deal is a fair deal."

"Who the hell are you?" said God.

"Dude," said the man, "what? You made me. Don't you know?"

"What hath I wrought, and all that shit," said God.

"Mystery to me, beyotch," said the man.

"..." said God.

"My bad, dude. Just playing."

Blink went the man.

Blink went the man. He was back.

"That sucked," said this guy. "My brother was back just long enough for me to remember what an asshole he is, but not long enough for me to forgive him for him being a huge asshole."

"Weak," said the man—the blinking in and out man. "Hey, God. What gives? Why do that to this poor schmuck?"

"Hey," said the schmuck.

"Sorry," said the man. "Just exaggerating for effect. Talking to God. You know how it is."

"No," said the schmuck. "God refuses to talk to me. Ever since I said some nasty shit to him when he killed my asshole brother."

God appeared, but didn't say anything. He, instead, made a head gesture. A "let's go this way" head gesture. The man and God went that way.

"What's up?" said the man.

"Nothing," said God. "I just really fucking hate that guy. You should have heard the shit he said about me after I offed his asshole brother."

"Epic," said the man.

"Totally," said God. God made like to high five with the man. The man followed through and tried for the high five, but God pulled his hand away and made a "too slow" gesture, where he ran his hands through his divine hair.

"So, but you brought me back before that schmuck and his asshole brother could get used to being around each other again, and now he's completely unsatisfied. I would like it if people were satisfied, you know? It would please me."

God, amused by the idea that other people—other things—could insist on their desires to assert their need for satisfaction, got this huge smile on his face. "Tell you what," said God. "I'll let everyone who has gone away come back, and I'll let them all come back for good. And all I ask in return is that you, my friend, go away and go away permanently. No Heaven for you. No Hell. No nothing. Just you blink out and you never know anything or think anything again. You be nothing and everyone else who ever was and ever will be gets to be something for all of eternity ever after. Nice deal, huh?"

"Not really," said the man. "Not really at all. I mean, me gone for good is me gone for good. I do this selfless thing and never get to enjoy it is one thing. I do this selfless thing and never get to police that you keep your promise is another thing. I do this selfless thing and never know if other people appreciate it, write maybe songs about me, or make statues. And maybe you don't even tell them that they are all back and all back forever because of something I did, too. And I get no glory in any case. Not a nice deal at all."

"Sure. Not really a nice deal from a self-involved perspective, maybe. But, good of the rest of the universe, multiverse, or whatever-wise? Pretty good deal."

The man chewed his big toenail. (He was limber and could reach.) "Will you make me a statue?" said the man.

"Me?" said God.

"Like, a Heavenly statue? A statue in Heaven?"

"No one will see it," said God. "Everyone will be out of Heaven and back on Earth."

"You will," said the man.

"I don't really have eyes," said God.

"You have a mouth," said the man.

"Sure," said God.

"And in that mouth, you have a tongue," said the man.

"Sure," said God.

"And with that tongue, you can caress the statue tip to toe. Caress it and experience it and know it," said the man.

"Sure," said God.

"And by knowing it, inform the universe in one way or another with it. With me. I will imbue the universe through the words that cross the tongue that caressed my statue," said the man.

"Umm," said God.

"Admit," said the man.

"I guess," said God. "I guess, sure."

"The I will always be, too. I'll do it," said the man. Blink went the man.

THIS MOUNTAIN I BUILT

I built a mountain in my backyard. With my own hands, I built a mountain in my backyard. With a shovel, and a wheelbarrow, and bag after bag of concrete, and cinder blocks and dirt, I built a mountain in my backyard.

Because I thought one belonged there.

When it was complete, my mountain reached up to the clouds. I watched as a snowcap formed on the top, vegetation crawled its way around and up, and as fauna took hold. I had really done something, making this mountain. I called my son over to ask him what he thought.

He looked up at it and said, "It's good."

I stared at my son. I stared at my boy, Sport, and couldn't speak. "It's good," was what he had said. I'd built a mountain in my backyard, and did it over a long holiday weekend. "It's good," is all he said. Me, I looked back at my mountain in all its grandeur, and I felt a little chorus of joyous voices begin to sing to my soul. Sport, he went off to drink from the hose.

My son is named Sport and he is a very young boy. He is nine years old, and he doesn't care for me. We have awkward conversations. An example would be like, I see him in the hallway, and he sees me, and we have to say something. There's no way we can walk by one another without saying *something,* so we do. I start with a question like, "Have you seen your mother lately?" And he'll respond.

He'll say: "I saw her at breakfast," maybe.

And it will just stop there. We'll nod and move on. That's what it's like.

I don't understand things, either. I don't understand why it is when we're in the car together, and I play a song by The Beatles, he tells me to turn it off. I don't understand how I have a person in my car who doesn't understand how much is absolutely beautiful and perfect about "Taxman. I don't understand why a person like that gets to ride in my car. And I have to let him. I have to, too. My wife has insisted. Every single time I've asked.

It was this: I was in my backyard, and I was lying face down in the hammock when it occurred to me that I needed to build a mountain there, in the spot just below me. I had dropped my beer can. It was on its side, right under me, and it was framed by the white, knotted threads of the hammock. It was half-full, and was spilling out into the grass, beer sinking into the dirt, leaving a film of off-white bubbles. I made my eyes squint tight, and focused hard on the bubbles, them all shining and clustered but slowly spreading out from a central pcak.

I noticed I was shaking my leg, and the hammock was swinging gently.

I told my wife about it immediately. I ran into the house to find her, and there she was, sitting at our computer, writing to a friend of hers from college. I went right up to her and I told her that I had had an important idea.

Something very important had occurred to me, and I needed to tell her all about it.

She held up a finger. Just one. She held it up, and I waited. She put down her finger, and finished typing her letter, or she found a good stopping place, or something, and then she swiveled in her chair and finally faced me.

"Okay," she said, staring at me. "Go ahead."

"I'm going to build a mountain in the backyard," I told her.

She swiveled back to the computer and resumed typing. "Okay," she said. "Involve Sport in that in some way."

I drove Sport and me to a hardware store. We went to one of the big ones on the edge of town. We went to one of those big, comprehensive, shelves-to-the-sky hardware stores, and we parked the car.

When we walked to the store, Sport would not hold my hand, even though he is a little boy, and little boys should hold their parents' hands when they walk through parking lots or any other place where there are moving cars.

A dog in the backseat of an economy class vehicle looked at us with a sidelong, low-eyed glance.

I have been made to understand that this is an expression dogs make in circumstances where they are unsure what is wrong with the people they are looking at. They know something is not right, and they are disappointed in the way things are going. This look you get from dogs sometimes is a sort of tsk.

I tried to grab my son's hand to mollify the dog, but Sport would have none of it.

Okay, aisles baffle me. I need to spend a long moment trying to orient myself whenever I enter any shop with more than ten numbered aisles. I need to familiarize myself with the hanging product guides and shelves that climb well beyond the tip of my and any other person's reach.

Sport is unfazed by this sensory overload. He is, when we shop together, compelled to wait for me to acquaint myself with our mercantile environment, but his cockeyed looks and bored-leg shuffles betray his annoyance. It's more accurate, though, to say that they betray his annoyance, and through them, he betrays me. He is daddy's little quisling.

At the store, we were helped by a man with an orange vest and a lazy eye.

"What's wrong with your eye?" Sport asked.

The man did not answer, but looked over at me. I smiled at him, and gave a shrug. He returned the shrug. Kids, we said through our shrugs. They just go ahead and say things, don't they?

"Some people just have messed up eyes," I told my son.

"Wow," said the man.

I told the man we needed some things because we were going to build a mountain in our backyard.

"Well," I said, "my backyard. I'm the one who paid for it, right son?"

Sport pulled a plastic army man—the one who is posed on his belly, looking through binoculars—out of his pocket, and deployed it next to a bin of screws.

And then, it happened again. The man, whose name was Dale, asked, "A backyard mountain? Just what sort of a things are you and your pop up to there, Sport?"

He called Sport by his name without first asking me if it was okay to do so. In fact, he had just guessed my son's name, like some sort of stage wizard. I told Dale I was very uncomfortable working with him because of his unnatural and possibly occult-based powers, and I asked to see another sales associate. He feigned confusion, but called over another fellow.

This new fellow suggested a wire base and plaster, but I dismissed the idea. I wanted something far more substantial inside my mountain. "This isn't going to be one of your fake backyard mountain mountains," I told him.

"A pyramid of cinder blocks?" he asked. And that was just the trick.

Sport was distant throughout the building process, possibly thinking about cartoons. When we loaded everything in the minivan, he didn't lift a finger—not a block of concrete or a thirty-pound bag. In the car, he sat next to the cans of paint without once engaging with them. "They'll make a heck of a mountain, won't they?" I asked. He sat and chewed on the tips of his fingernails. "You will," I told the bag of plaster belted into the passenger seat. "You'll make a heck of a mountain."

I built the mountain over the next four days. Neighbors came by to watch and to complain, but I kept at it. Sport chose to ignore it. He flooded anthills, instead, and drove his plastic cars around the bushes, playing that every main branch was a street and every smaller branch shooting from the main was an alley. He never once chased off anyone.

The neighbors, when they looked at my mountain-in-progress, expressed to me that they thought it might block views in unseemly, not-so-neighborly ways. They wondered aloud and en masse if there would have to be an emergency neighborhood committee meeting to discuss this whole mountain thing.

By day four, though, the mountain was so large, most of the houses near us were gone. They had been subsumed by it and its massiveness. The neighborhood was mostly gone, vanished, and our house sat at the foot of the mountain. I went to sleep that night happy.

In the dark of that evening, God appeared to me, burning like a star, at the foot of my bed. He said, "Tomorrow you will take your only son, your boy Sport, to a place on the mountain that I will show you, and you will make of him a burnt offering to the Lord your God." I, half asleep and surprised to find myself awestruck and devoted to a God I had never really given much thought to, figured yes. We surprise ourselves at the big moments, don't we?

I took my boy and we went to climb the mountain. I told my wife I had decided to take a few extra days off from my job and go camping with my son. We gathered up two old, musty sleeping bags, the green one and the brown one, in case we needed to stop for a night before we reached the place the Lord had chosen for the altar of sacrifice. And I packed a tent, in case the altar was high up in the mountain, so high that the weather could affect us.

In the basement, I found my old Boy Scout hatchet. Its blade was quite dull, but I set to work on it with a whetstone and soon it was fine and sharp. I took bungee cords from the back of the minivan, figuring I would need them to bind my son to the altar.

And, we started up the mountain. I was walking, he was running to keep up with my longer strides. We found a trail in the ferns and trees, and followed it. "See," I said. "A trail. I thought of everything."

It was early afternoon, and a slightly chilly day. Mushrooms grew in the damp, and I told Sport which ones I thought he shouldn't eat, though I knew nothing of mushrooms. I told him what plants I thought he should avoid, too, to keep from getting a rash. And I told him not to eat anything that looked like a berry. I hummed "Across the Universe" to myself, and tried to get Sport to join in.

Sport pulled bracken ferns from the dirt, and pretended they were spears. He threw them, and the pointy, heavy root leading them to the ground a few feet ahead. Tree roots stuck up in the elevating path, and we used them as steps. And we climbed all afternoon, not speaking much to one another.

I gave Sport granola when he looked hungry, and he sipped water from a plastic canteen I had bought for him at an Army surplus store.

"Maybe some time soon, you and I will go fishing," I told Sport. "My dad and I went fishing a couple of times. I think I still have the poles in the basement."

"Where?" asked Sport.

"Behind the box full of balls and gloves and lawn darts. I caught a fish once, one of those flat ones. We laid it down on the rocks in front of us, and watched it try to breath through its mouth, though it couldn't. I even tried to pet it, but when you stroke them the wrong way, it feels prickly."

Sport pulled a low branch down from a tree and hit the trunk with it. It was wet, but still splintered and shattered.

"Good talk, son," I said.

When the sun was setting, we made a small fire, and decided to spend the night. We made hot dogs and s'mores. Sport fell asleep in the tent, and I followed a little later. I considered praying, but couldn't come up with a prayer that seemed up to the task of being the prayer one prays when one is climbing a mountain to sacrifice one's son to God. All my prayer drafts sounded like a grace offered at a dinner table by an on-the-spot boyfriend brought home for the first time to a Thanksgiving dinner who is surprised by the depth of faith of his girlfriend's family.

We reached the spot on the afternoon of the second day, the clearing provided by God, with a fallen tree and a view of our cul-de-sac. I bound my son's hands and feet with the bungee cord, made the fire, and prepared to sacrifice Sport, just as the Lord had commanded me. I gagged my son, too, because he was making a bit of a racket.

As I raised the hatchet and lifted Sport's head so his neck was open to me, the Angel of God appeared. He stood very near to me, so near I could feel his frozen breath. I paused, and we stared at one another.

I caressed Sport's neck with my thumb, up and down and in little circles around the Adam's apple, hoping it would stop his squirming, hoping the physical contact would calm him.

My hand remained raised, and the Angel of God and me? We just stared each other for a while.

"Well?" he said.

APPLE

Witch (Or Crone, or weird sister, or whatever it is you and your kind call yourselves),

I tend to think of myself as the sort of person who respects an individual or groups right to self-identify, and I apologize for being dismissive there in my greeting, but at the same time, I find myself being so very frustrated by the situation that leads me to write this letter that I'm having trouble being courteous. Or even having the wherewithal to go back and edit out rudeness. Trust, then, that the curtness of that opening speaks to my anger, which is causing me to communicate in a way that is completely out of character for me.

I'm writing you with a serious complaint. I would like to complain about the effectiveness, or rather the lack of effectiveness of the poisoned apple I purchased from you. Or rather, the apple worked, in a way, but it did not work the way you told me it would work. Not exactly. That's what I would like to complain about.

Let me first remind you of who I am. My name is D—. My girlfriend is L—. I purchased a poisoned apple from you six months ago, in order to feed it to L—, because I wanted her to sleep for a while. I wanted some time away from our fighting. I wanted some time away from all the arguing. I wanted some time away from feeling like everything I said was being analyzed for what seem to be inevitable flaws in my thinking. But, only some time. Only some time is what I wanted. That's what you told me I could have. Some time.

You will recall we met on the bus. I was on my way to work. You stepped on the bus and did not pay. You did not look up, just walked by the driver. You were disheveled and I took you for homeless. I read my book and did my best to disappear, to make the empty seat next to me disappear, but you found me anyway.

You smell like urine, witch. I'm sure you are aware of that. I'm sorry to bring it up. It's true. You smell like urine. You, in a blue terry cloth robe. You have not washed your hair in a long time, possibly ever. You stumble and sort of buzz when you walk—as if a nest of wasps lives in your mouth. And you sat down next to me.

I considered just getting up and moving to the back of the bus. You smell bad and mutter under your breath, and I took you for crazy, too, and just wanted to get away from you. Just read my book and go to work, and ignore you is all I intended to do. But you spoke to me.

"She's always on you, you think," is what you said. I kept reading. You were talking—to yourself, I was sure. "You think she'll always be like that. You think she is embarrassed by you."

"I'm sorry," I said.

"She's smarter than you," you said.

"Who are you talking to? Are you talking to me?" I said.

"I know what you want," you said.

"Don't talk to me," I said. "I don't want to talk to you."

"I can help you," you said. "I can give you something that will help. I can make L— sleep. Sleep as long as you want her to. I can help you."

I went back to ignoring you. It seemed the best thing to do. To forget that you had just said her name.

Do you remember me, now? You went nattering on and on. I pulled the cord, but you said it wasn't my stop. You knew it wasn't my stop and told me so. I tried to get up, but you blocked me. You touched my shoulder and my legs stopped working.

"I can. I can help you," you said, and blew a rancid breath into my face. I reeled. I turned my head away. I gagged.

But I believed you.

"We'll get off at the next stop," you said, and I agreed.

We got off the bus together, and you led me to an alley. It was morning. It really was morning, but in the alley it was dusk. The asphalt was worn, broken up in places. I followed you, tripping on the uneven ground. The brick walls of the alley were covered with graffiti.

You moved so very gracefully. A cat met us near a tent made of a green plastic tarp. You grabbed an end and pushed me in.

It smelled of garbage inside. You had half-empty Styrofoam containers, old blankets, and a cooking pot. Old coats. It smelled bitter and sour. You sat on a milk crate. There was a bone in the pot, brown and blackening marrow at the cracked end. Two canteens hung from the tent's wooden structure. There was a photo, bubbled, and browned, melted and in it all I could make out was an eye. The rest of the portrait had burned away. The cat sat next to me on a blanket, and I was on my knees.

"This will cost you, but not that much," you said. You dug through the containers and pulled out an apple.

It was a shiny green apple. It was unspoiled, unbruised. New and fresh.

"You will feed this to L—," you said. "If you feed even just a single bite to her, she will fall into a deep, deep sleep. And then, you can have your time. She will still be yours. She will not leave. She will just sleep, and she won't wake up. You can care for her, then. Dress her how you want. She will not need to eat. She will not age. She will just sleep. Sleep," you said, and you smiled.

You have rotten teeth.

"What if I want her to wake up?" I asked.

"The kiss of her true love will wake her up. Simple. Kiss her. And she will wake up. Keep the apple as long as you want. It will not spoil until you cut into it. Use it when you are ready."

I purchased the apple. Again you blew in my face, and again I wobbled. I left. When I was back at the bus stop, on my way to work—your home was only half way there—I went back to not believing you. I told myself I purchased the apple from you because it was a good deed. It was charity. You were right. It was very affordable. I put the apple in my bag. I left it in my bag.

L— and I are together and she puts up with me. This is all I ask. She puts up with my inability to remember making plans. She puts up with me even though I don't know what day of the week it is. She puts up with the fact that I will sometimes in a restaurant butter a roll, and then quickly, but not slyly, wipe the excess butter off my knife with my pinky and lick it. She scolds me for doing that if anyone else is around. She is, as you noted, embarrassed by me.

She puts up with me even though I am not very bright. Sometimes, something will occur to me and I will tell L— about it, and she will look at me with a look of genuine pity. And she shows me why I am wrong. She will remind me of the obvious thing I have forgotten that makes the thing that just occurred to me completely wrong. Am I making sense? She knows why I'm wrong, and she tells me why, and I listen and see that she is correct. And I take that thing that has occurred to me, and I throw it out my brain's window, and it lands on the street as my brain and I drive off.

L—'s long red hair is as beautiful as it is possible for hair to be, I think.

L—'s eyes are as smart as a pair of eyes can appear to be.

That's why I need L— around. That's why I can't ask her to leave, and wouldn't let her if she wanted to leave. That's why putting her to sleep made so much sense.

Though, as I said, I didn't believe the apple would actually put her to sleep.

We were talking about something—oil prices, maybe, or where we would go if we won a free trip on a game show of some sort. I had thought they were going to go down after the war, or maybe that I'd like to see Africa. She told me either that oil production had hit its peak, or that Africa was in turmoil, and I knew she was right. And I knew I was wrong.

And I just felt bad. Friends were over, and they laughed. Where would I be without L—, they wondered. The Sudan with a gun to his head, she told them. Or away in Iraq, fighting "terrorism," she maybe told them, making quotes with her fingers.

Maybe we were discussing the fastest route home from downtown? I am poor with directions.

Our friends left. L— called her dad, and they talked about his patients. (He's a doctor.) L— told him about her classes. (She's a grad student, studying history.) I went to my bag and took out my book. And the apple fell out.

L— likes a snack before bed, so I cut up the apple and put it on a plate, and added a little lump of peanut butter. I told her I wasn't hungry.

She had a little bite of a slice of the apple. Then she had the rest. I read and she lay next to me and drifted off. I got up and put the plate in the kitchen. I read. She was snoring, just a little. I fell asleep.

It's like the world forgot about her. Her friends don't call. Her family doesn't call. The school hasn't called. It's like, except for the fact that she's there, in our bed, asleep, she just went away. She fell out of the big book of human history.

Her friends don't recognize me on the street. They walk right by me without acknowledging me. And some of them look right at me!

I woke up the next day, and she was asleep. She mumbled, but did not wake up when I shook her.

I started to believe. To really believe.

When she is asleep, I love her more than any other time. Her face is rounded, a little puffier. It doesn't smile, but it also doesn't frown.

She is, when awake, full of energy, and sometimes it exhausts me to try to keep up. Asleep, her body sinks and rises. It does not vibrate so quickly. Her rhythms are predictable. She is, when asleep, not so dangerous to me.

Months she was like that. Months she slept. Our room was dark and warm. For the first month, the air in our room was thick and comfortable. I had a fan spinning in the corner. On rare occasions, she shifted. Mostly, she lay facing my side of the bed, the comforter up around her head, her face the only thing visible. I woke up every morning and turned to her and stared at her. Light leaked in through the corner of the window, a little spot missed by our heavy curtains. I didn't want to get up. I didn't want to leave her. I just wanted to sleep, too.

For a while I did. I spent a week just there with her. I called in sick. I stayed in bed with L—, for long, happy days without arguments. Without fights. Without proof of my essential ignorance of all things.

It was nice. I would sometimes roll over her, and pull back the covers to stare at the long, white curve of her back. I would trace a line from mole to freckle to nape of neck.

But soon it was clear I needed to leave her and get back to work.

Three months went well, but then I missed her. So, I kissed my L— to wake her up.

She won't wake up, Witch. She won't wake up. She won't wake up. She won't wake up.

I kiss her and kiss her, but she won't wake up.

Bedsores. My life has become filled with the concern over and caring for of the bedsores that are opening on my L—. She has pressure ulcers on her back. I turn her over every night to give them a chance to heal. I go to work, and she rolls back into her favorite position, facing my side of the bed.

I wash her every couple of days.

She does not need to eat. You were right about that. I tried to feed her once, massaged her throat to get her to swallow, but she didn't. The applesauce just sat in her mouth until I cleaned it out.

She doesn't age, but her hair grows. Her fingernails grow. Her toenails grow. I clip them. But I have left her hair to grow as it wishes. I'd probably just mess it up if I tried to cut it.

I don't sleep anymore. I haven't slept in a month and a half.

I've started smoking again. I sit in a chair all night, and watch her sleep, and I smoke cigarettes. Can she get lung cancer from the second hand smoke? She still breathes. Her chest expands and contracts under the comforter.

I kiss her and she doesn't wake up.

I get the twist, you know. I get the kiss of her true love thing that is going on. You have tricked me, but it's not subtle, witch. I get it. I get the gag.

Wake her up.

I have returned to your alley many times and haven't found you. I take the bus around town, and don't find you. I know what you're doing. I know you're punishing me.

Wake her up.

And give me a refund. I know, caveat emptor. I'm familiar. But I think, legally speaking, I have a case.

I'll leave this letter in "your" alley. I'll wait for you to respond. I'll wait for satisfaction.

Wake her up, witch. I'll track you down. I'll find you eventually. I will. Count on it.

Wake her up.

D—

DEFENESTRATION,
A LOVE STORY

That whole thing about glass flowing because it's liquid, mostly, and how when you see warps in the window and a warp to the look of the world outside a window, you are looking at glass flowing? That thing is complete bullshit.

That whole thing about birds running into your windows because they see inside and think that life inside your home is way better than the lives they have on the outside world, so they run into your windows hoping to break through and when they get in, because of the great amount of effort they have gone through or expended or whatever, you'll let them live with you or be forced to give your lives to them and take their places as birds out in the open world while they get to carry on as people living people lives? That's complete bullshit, too.

That whole thing about how the safest thing to wear in a warzone is a suit made of bulletproof glass from the windows of the Pope's car because not only is the glass bulletproof, but it has also been blessed by God and God's servants on Earth to be impenetrable by all the many kinds of projectiles the evil species called Humanity chooses to project at one another, and how you can buy a suit like that on the internet for your friends and relatives who live or fight or both live and fight in a warzone? That's a bullshit scam and someone should go to prison for it.

But when they say the best way to prove to someone that you love her or him is to throw her or him out of a window, that's the truth. People who say that are telling you the God's honest truth.

At one time, the proper method of political assassination in the city of Prague was defenestration—the tossing of one's leader out of an open window.

At a much later time, but not the time that is now, the proper way to show love was to toss the one you love out of a window. Maybe it seems odd now. But then, you loved and you longed and you grabbed hold of the one you wanted to be with and you picked them up and you threw them out the window.

You understand?

Of course you don't. How could you? The world was the world. The world now seems like the world— seems like it to you—but the world never really is the world or it always is. You love someone, you write him a letter. You love someone, you write her a song. You love someone, you open a window, grab hands, feet, backs, give a swing, let go, and away from you they fly.

It was not a fever. It was not a culture gone insane. We were sure about what we were doing. We were not out of our heads except out of our heads in love and that is what that was.

That's what that was. You're missing the point. You sit in your chair and you miss the point entirely, is all. That's all. Sitting and missing. And it's almost like you want to. It's almost like you mean to.

A lot of folks miss the point these days. I blame the way we don't understand about what life was like back when you risked yourself all the time just by living and by maybe being the target of someone's love when love and gravity were so completely intertwined. Risked it by going to work in any building over two stories, I mean. Risk is a thing that is beautiful, that's what I think.

A window is a thing that is beautiful, that's what I think. Look at this one between the sky and us. What if we opened it up and we just threw you out? What if we saw what that would be like? Do you think you'd understand it better? Because I did, at some point—I lived in a world where the windows were open and the sky was filled with the shouts and the screams of the loved. Can you imagine such a thing? A world with love in the great, blue, open, cloudless, empty, shining, stupid, pointless sky?

At the time, we were like: This is a window. It's used for all kinds of things, but the thing I like best to do with it is to throw people out of it. That's what I think is the best of all things to do with a window. And as I have said so many times before, what I mean when I throw you out of a window is I love you. That's what I mean and what I like to use a window for. Got me? This thing is hardwired into me is what I want you to know.

Windows and skies and bodies in the air, my friend. Windows and skies and love. See how I mean this? See how you out in the air and falling and falling is me in love with you? What's the best way to love? says the crowd. Tossing you out of a window is my answer. Who do we toss out a window? says the crowd. The ones that we love and the ones that we want to express that love to, I respond. When do we hit the ground? asks the crowd. The moment we know that love is real, I say. But do we know it's real because we hit the ground, or do we not hit the ground until the moment we really, truly feel like, Yes, it is real and we are loved? asks the crowd. I don't know how to answer that question. I think it's both, but I don't know if that is an answer that makes sense to anyone but me and the one I love, who has hit the ground already and doesn't have an answer to offer anymore.

We are loved. Have I told you that? Have I mentioned it? I hope so. I hope I've remembered to say that. It's the most important thing of all.

So, a tribute to all the window washers who make our sight of love in the air so very, very clear. Let's toast to the man with the squeegee and the pail of soapy water, who likes to be up high and on a platform with a winch that is good for making a platform rise up on the outside of a building and then also lowers it down—though the rising is the best thing for the platform. Lowering down is for falling, and falling fast and faster. Lowering down slow is a mockery of love. Our best to the ones who like to clean the high, dizzyingly high windows that let us fall to love's real finish line.

GRACKLES

MISSION STATEMENT
Our street gang is Grackles and we're not afraid of cops.

LOCATION
Alleyways and under bridges and sometimes in cornfields, where its us pulling tassels and laying on our backs in the rows.

OUTFITS
Large, conical paper hats that look more than just "quite stylish" but really very, very much better than that.

ACTIVITIES
Homecoming Dance Massacre, 2003; Random Jackass Mugging Week, 2001; Life Choices Open Mic Night, 2004; Inspiration Removal Sing-A-Long, 2004, Year of Year Off, 2002; Limber-cise on the 44 to Ballard, 2005; Loose Clothing Pull-Away Month, Upcoming.

DIET
Blackberry and vanilla yogurt smoothie and grilled chicken sandwich.

ANSWER TO MOST QUESTIONS
So's your old man and mother, both.

TIME LIKELY TO BE SPENT IN PRISON BY AGE 23
Many years. Maybe nine or something? Maybe.

ACCOMPLISHMENTS
MacArthur Genius Grants all around, made an old
man cry with rage, sometimes have a remarkable
thought or two.

DEATH
In the fall. Always, always, always in the fall.

SLEEP UNDERGROUND

In the evenings, when the heat becomes too much—
which it always does in the height of summer—he digs
himself into the dirt to sleep. It's cooler underground. He
has been doing so for two years.

It was on the fifth night of the current summer, and
in the earth, he met a very pleasant mole.

The mole sniffed at him—this large mammal with
a thin, acrid smell of cooling sweat over him—and wondered if he was there to eat the mole. But, no—the little boar mole sensed no real danger from the big, doz-
ing mammal. The gentle way the man moved, dug,
breathed—the mole sensed that the man did not have
the predator's aspect, the predator's veil of alertness,
hunger, danger. The mole decided he was safe near the
creature, and decided to allow it to share his space.

In the mornings, from a tower, a sound: a bell rings. A
church bell rings seven times.

He digs himself out of the soil. He rubs the dirt
from his arms. He shakes the dirt loose from his hair. He
unplugs the dirt from his ears. He spends a moment just
staring, staring. She comes out to the yard. She hands
him a cup of coffee, and he sips and he walks to the bathroom to shower. It's tough, sometimes, getting motivated
in the morning. It's frustrating. Just an hour more sleep

could do so much good. Just a single hour. How petty, the sun. How rude, the bell of the church.

Water falls down his chest and races to a darkening pool below. The shower drain needs snaking again. He will have to remember to borrow the snake from his neighbor. The tub fills up slowly and the water just won't swirl away, sometimes even for as long as an hour after he has finished. The mud has to be wiped down, and she expects him to do it when he gets home from work. And he is happy to do it, as it is his mud. His teeth coat with the mud, and grass roots lodge between them; he flosses the roots away, and spits them in the small, blue, plastic garbage can below the bathroom sink. The can needs to be emptied weekly into the yard waste bin. She does not abide recyclable goods going unrecycled.

He sweeps the dust from the floor before he leaves for work, if he has the time. It's the least he can do.

In high summer, like now, this process—this getting-up process—is harder than early or late summer. Sod is cool, and he would prefer not to sweat. They live in a city that is hot and wet for far too long every year. She loves it. He would prefer to wind his body around the roots of a favorite tree and spend the season living off stored body fat. But she will have none of it. She will not follow.

She loves the summer. She unleashes herself from his plodding rhythm when the sky gets open and bright, and the leaves turn green, and the lawns turn green and then burn brown. She teaches dance classes in the park all summer long—modern, tap, salsa and swing, from 6am – 9pm. She is, to his dismay, a morning person.

A morning person. Who can figure. They met in

the evening. He thought it was indicative.

Two years ago, it was the heat of the summer that drove him underground. The heat interrupted his sleep. The sweat on the back of his neck itched. The heat wouldn't let him escape to his dreams. It kept him at the edge of consciousness all night.

He sleeps best wrapped in blankets. In the heat, it was impossible. He kicked them off. The absence of weight woke him. He pulled them back. He sweated and kicked them off. He stayed awake all night. She slept fine.

And then he thought about the ground. It was cooler underneath. It was tighter, and cooler, and much more pleasant than having to—every single night—fight with heat in order to sleep.

So, he tried it. He told her he was going to go outside and dig himself into the dirt, and he was going to sleep there, and would come back in the morning.

It worked wonderfully. He clawed down, and down, and covered himself over in dirt, and clawed a little farther to a nice, cool spot, and drifted away. He thought everyone should try it. He told everyone. He made it a point to tell everyone.

He is a contingent employee at a data entry company. He sits before a screen of baby blue, at a blond wood table curved for his comfort, in a chair formed round at the spine for his comfort, at a keyboard bent like a stone bridge for the comfort and health of the thin tendons in his wrists. He types and types, and he does not like his job.

A man named Morris comes over to his desk, followed by a man named Doran. They are friends, and friends of his, of a sort. "Why," Morris asks, "are you still here, Casey? Seems like you could've left or something by now. Gotten a new job? Found a full-time employment type situation?"

"Sure," says Doran. "It's crazy for you to still be here. You've been here longer than me," he says, and laughs. He has himself a really good laugh.

The man types, and smiles, and they can see a little dirt still stuck between his teeth.

"Right, well," says Morris. "Catch you later, buddy." He says the lay part of later for a really long time. Like: laaaaaaaay-ter. Doran has himself another really good laugh, and then he punches the man in the shoulder. It makes a pop that seems a little like a joke at first, but then doesn't quite.

He sits at his desk and he types. And then he notices a spontaneous erection. An erection unprovoked by human hands or visual stimulation or chemical facilitation. It's just there in his lap, like when he was a teenager, and the darn things appeared out of nowhere. For him to enjoy. And admire. An act of a compassionate and loving God.

It brightens his day.

He told her once he would like to impregnate her the day the next snowfall covers the ground and that it— the pregnancy—would go like this: he'd wrap himself around her shoulders all winter long, and she would go under the dirt with him. Her feet would get gummy, he mentioned, and she would stick in place until it was time for the very blessed event, and out would come their son. They would feed it, and keep it moist, and it would grow up and, probably, become a gardener of some sort. Maybe one of the ones who carves animals from hedges. A topiary gardener.

She told him he did not understand the process of human reproduction if he thinks that's the way it goes. She suggested to him he might be thinking about frogs, not people.

In the morning, she wakes with her arms around a pillow. A fan is running, and it is more than enough for her. She is thinking about getting a dog: a big, square-headed, square-shouldered, dumb-as-a-post boy. A goopy-eyed boy that she will have to fuss over with a tissue. She likes to go online and look at the dogs available at the local shelter, and she takes time to check out each new male, seeing if maybe it is the one that will fit the bill.

She is intolerant of small, nervous dogs with long hair. She wants no part of a dog that needs to be combed or sculpted. She wants no part of a dog that needs to be coddled or fussed over.

She is not sure why she is still making him coffee, but has decided that she will continue for a little while longer. Not forever, though. Once, she told him.

She said to him, "This isn't going to go on forever."

"No, I know," he said.

"You can maybe start to make your own coffee," she said.

"Is that what you meant?" he said.

"What else?" she said.

"No, just that," he said.

"I don't even drink coffee," she said. "Doesn't help me wake up."

She will name the dog Oscar. Or Roscoe. Something old sounding. Something that would make people imagine him in a bowler hat or a straw boater. Or hugging a banjo.

At work, Morris comes back with Doran behind. Morris has a very tiny, rounded face like a butter knife. Like a bunny. Doran spends all his time peering out from behind Morris, and is pretty much just half there. "You sure do work hard, buddy," Morris says. "Know what that makes you?" he asks. "Nutso!"

"Ha, nutso," says Doran.

"Abso-fucking-lutely fuck-o," says Morris. And he swirls his index finger, which he has pointed at his head, like if he could put his finger through his ear and into his skull, he could swirl his brain, and also know what it was like to be fuck-o, just like the man sitting before him, typing.

"I'm just kidding you, buddy," he says.

"Oh, sure," says Doran. "You're all right. Hey, this fellow is all right," he says, a little louder, over his shoulder, to no one.

Someone, an office assistant in a green tie hanging an inch too long past the waist of his pants, walks by, and Doran looks at him, and looks at the man at the desk, and gives the tie man a thumbs up and says, "This guy here is totally all right, you know?"

The office assistant knocks on the wall as he walks by. Three times he knocks. And then he crosses himself.

"Don't mind that," says Morris. "Some of them just do that for luck. Office assistants are very superstitious. We should call the comptroller over here. The comptroller totally scares the office assistants. Much more than you do. You're just, you know, eccentric. The comptroller is a real bastard!"

At lunch, he goes up to the observation deck. He sits alone on a bench and stares out from the deck, and looks to the park, where his wife is teaching her dance lessons. He has a sandwich, and drinks a diet soda, and watches, and can sort of see her.

The observation deck has coin-operated telescopes. He takes a couple of quarters from his pocket and aims the telescope to the park, to a small gathering that he figures is his wife and her class. He looks through the telescope, and drops the quarters in the coin slots to get the maximum amount of time looking at his wife. It is cold metal, rough to the touch, cold on his eye, swiveling in a small arc, disinterested in a full range of motion, and it clicks his time away.

He sees her and her class. Tick tick. They are gathered together in a circle, doing an exercise she does with her students on the first day of a new class. Tick tick.

"You may be nervous about dancing in front of people," she says. "This may make you uncomfortable, being this vulnerable. So gather in a circle. Everyone put your arms over the shoulders of the person next to you. And when the music starts to play, we'll all dance together."

And that's what they do. They spin together. They cross one leg in front of the other in long steps, in time to the music. They turn in a big circle, around the park. And soon their arms slip down, and they are holding hands. And soon their hands slip away and they are dancing alone.

Through the telescope, they look like a Matisse. Tick tick. They look like clothed versions of the dancers in that Matisse painting. The ground is just as green. The skin is just as pink and orange, the sky is just as blue.

There bodies are just as twisted into one another. The hills are just as round. Their shoulders are just as round. And she is the strongest part of the circle. Tick tick. They pivot with her. They move with her. They twirl at her behest. She pushes. She pulls. She shines. Tock. The end of the telescope goes black.

He is called into his supervisor's office.

"So, Casey."

"Yes?"

"How goes?"

"Just fine."

"Just fine?"

"Just fine."

"Okay, then. See you later."

"Thank you, sir."

He is called in to the office every day, and they have the same conversation. The supervisor tells his own supervisors that he calls Casey into his office to "put him on notice." They agree that Casey needs very much to be "put on notice," because there is something about him that "needs addressing." They are thinking long and hard about it. They are thinking long and hard about what to do about Casey.

He goes back to his desk and resumes typing.

"Well," says Morris, "how about this?"

"Yeah, look here," says Doran.

"Here we are back at the desk," says Morris.

"Typing," says Doran.

"Entering the data," says Morris.

"Oh, yeah," says Doran. "Data is being entered."

Morris and Doran high-five.

The man scratches behind his ear, and pulls out a small lump of mud he missed in the shower. Doran scampers away, and Morris backs off slowly, smiling.

The mole and his sow will sometimes cozy up to him because, though he has gone underground to avoid the heat, the little ones are sometimes cold. He doesn't so much mind. They are small and radiate very little warmth. And they are friendly about it. They bring him worms.

He has told her all about the moles, and all about the dirt, and has asked her to come down with him some night, but she won't do it. She thinks they should, at the dinner table, not discuss sleeping below the ground, but instead, maybe, discuss the state of their relationship.

"Summer ends soon," he says.

"And, then?" she asks.

"And then I'll come back up. But, now…"

He picks at the green beans on his plate. She drinks a glass of milk, swallowing most of it in one gulp—one aggressive gulp.

He points the living room fan at himself.

When he is dug in, she calls her mother to ask for advice, but her mother has none. "At no point did your father do anything remotely like this," she says. "Why would you think I would know what to do?"

"You're right," she says. "You're right."

"Maybe just wait until winter, and for now indulge him. It's his version of the seven year itch."

"Probably," she says. "Probably."

"When are we going to get some grandchildren,

that's what I want to know. We're not getting any younger. And neither are you."

"Yes, mother. None of us are getting any younger, no matter how hard we try. Well. Unless we really, really try hard."

He gets home. They have a silent dinner. They read in the living room, silently. It is cooler this evening than it has been in a while.

"It's cooler this evening," she says.

He rubs the back of his neck.

They turn on the radio and listen to a program of old dance music from the 40s and 50s. She taps her foot. And swivels her neck. He finds the clarinets distracting and has trouble reading his book.

"The supervisor asked to see me today," he says. This is his joke. She usually mocks worry when he says this. Usually.

"And how did that go?" she says.

"Swimmingly," he says. "It went positively swimmingly. We've really come to an understanding."

"What sort of an understanding?" she says.

"He's got his eye on me, and I'm aware that he's got his eye on me," he says.

"Everybody wins," she says. "So, tonight?"

"Maybe tomorrow," he says. "Still a little—"

"Warm," she says.

On toward evening, he changes into his pajamas. She follows him out into the backyard. He sits down next to the sand-pale birch tree, the one with the loose dirt near it. She leans down and kisses him goodnight, and he leans up and kisses back. "See you in the morning," he says.

She names the dog Clyde. Clyde is a brindled, lunk-headed boxer, and he is a rescue. In the shelter, they say his name is Alonso, but she has her mind made up, knows that he is Clyde, and does not hesitate to rename him. On their first night together, after discovering that he can sit, and shake, and speak ever so abruptly, she sits down next to him, stares into his eyes, and says, "Clyde." She says it over and over. "Clyde. Clyde. Clyde. You are Clyde."

Clyde stares at her. He seems to be okay with the name change. He seems to have good coping skills. He seems to adapt.

"Okay? Clyde," she says.

He finds that he has nothing to say to the dog, so he doesn't. He follows his evening routine, and eventually retires.

He digs himself down, scuffling through the dirt with his hands. The moon and grass and trees disappear. She disappears.

Later, Clyde scratches at the back door, and she lets him out to run. Clyde explores the yard after marking a tree. He finds the soft dirt where Casey sleeps. He snuffles around it, pulls bits of loose soil away with his paws. It wakes him up. It scares the moles.

This happens every night for a week.

Casey says to her: "Will you please tell your dog not to dig up my bed?"

She responds: "Tell him? Tell my dog? And how do you propose I do that? We speak a very different language."

"You know what I mean," he says, wiping little bits of asparagus stalk into the garbage can with his fork.

"Please."

She goes into the living room, where Clyde is splayed out on the couch. "Who's my boy?" she asks. "Who's my baby boy?"

Work remains pretty much the same, except the days feel shorter as the days begin to get shorter and the leaves on the trees change color just at the tips. The brindle boxer follows her to the dance lessons, and sometimes joins in, getting down in a ready-to-play, shoulders down, butt up in the air position. When the dancers move side to side, Clyde fakes left, goes right, fakes right, goes left, fakes left, goes left, and runs beneath archways made of legs. At lunch, Casey watches.

And at night he digs himself down. She stands above him. She waits and wonders. She stamps a foot over him. She stamps, and then rocks a little, and does a dance. She starts with a simple box step, and then goes into a two-step above him. She has the music in her head, a Texas swing number that was on the radio just before he went to the bathroom to brush his teeth. Just before she followed him up to get ready for bed. She hears the song so clearly. So she dances to it. She dances her two-step. She can hear the fiddle, and she can hear the bass. And most of all, she can hear the lap steel guitar. She dances with the fingers of the lap steel guitar player.

TEENAGE MOTORCYCLE & LOVE TRAGEDY STORY

His neck snapped when he hit the pavement, but I swear it was the broken heart that killed him.

He lay down his bike on the final turn knowing it was his race to lose. The other bikes—behind him by a length as wide as is the width of the visual range of a person like you or me or someone else—shimmered into fading, mirage-like objects, and went out, and then gone. Nothing. The crowd and track and stands and checkered flag went next, and it was only then me and him and his still-rumbling, laying-down-on-a-white-expanse-of-fea-tureless-nothing ground motorcycle.

I ran out and grabbed hold of the broken body he was vacating. I stroked up and down and side to side on his face, bumping over his nose once a trip. He had eyes that weren't looking anywhere. And they were open. And they were moisture dense. And they were brown, because a boy has eyes that are brown. In all situations, a boy has eyes that are brown. In all versions of reality, a boy has eyes that are brown. Always, a boy has eyes that are brown.

See me, my hands on the sides of his face and my knees on the ground and my hair moving around like the wind is heavy and dramatic. See me in a skirt and a windbreaker that looks just like his windbreaker, because it's the windbreaker he gave me when I broke his heart and is his windbreaker, not just a windbreaker that looks just like his windbreaker.

See me crying tears of joy because, like he should, he died for the love of me.

You find bones and sedatives in a shoebox behind the shed. You wonder about the bones—bird bones, swallow bones—and swallow the sedatives one little night at a time. The nights are so little, like they are less than half the nights that used to be. The sedatives are strong and quick and you wake up right on time.

I make a star pattern of the bones that you gave me. That place where pill-taking creates happiness is somewhere I can't get to—a state a couple of states away that no one will hitchhike me to for fear of prosecution. That's how me and the pills don't meet. You? Better. So you take the pills and I don't.

I wish you were real. You wish it as well.

Trouble is magnified by the fact that we see him in the halls at school and decide he's for us, but can't choose between you and me when we both call dibs simultaneously.

Trouble is just trouble. He's just him. He's just a Johnny, like all the other Johnny's, because only in this world are you and me and Johnny.

We make more trouble of it, though, because making trouble of it is probably the only thing left to do here.

Let's make a fire in the trash can. Let's give our skirts to flames in the Girl's Room and run. Let's feel the last bits of it.

I'm tenderer there than you. You have your tenderness in places only imagined.

Let's ask Johnny for a cigarette and see if he will light it for us, or see if he is predisposed to letting us light the thing ourselves, and then decide if it means something or if it's just the way he is feeling at the time—maybe petulant, maybe hard—and make nothing of it.

Because why make things of things? Why ever in the world make things of things? What would be the kind of reasoning for that?

The shoebox has a crayoned name on it. In black and blue outlines, it's a box with a name that names Johnny.

Typical.

Johnny-from-a-long-time-ago Johnny. Johnny from the last of the last of the last of the folks in the neighborhood Johnny.

We remember Johnny.

I remember Johnny.

Oh, Johnny.

Let's make Johnny think we like him. Let's make Johnny fight for us. Let's make Johnny into the Johnny's of forever ago Johnny like there's nothing but the way to be and the way to act and the way to feel and the way to remember Johnny. That Johnny. That lovely, lovely Johnny.

I'll grab the booze from the liquor cabinet and we'll sneak over to his house. He lives on his own, no matter what his age mentions about his living arrangements.

Let's knock on a window. Let's flirt through glass.

Oh, God, please, let's flirt through glass. Let's hold the bottle to the window. You take the pills maybe out of the hem of our skirt. You shake them out in your palm like an offer to a pill-sot god of the old school variety. Like a god of drunken revelry. Like a god of determined, desperate silence.

Oh, gods. Let's fuck Johnny.

We hatched. A skull expelled us. Or a volcano erupted us. Or a river gathered us together like drifting wood flowing and catching against a rock.

Who knows. Here we are. That's enough.

It's just a frenzy of talk about talk, isn't it? You, God, my imaginary friend. You, God, my imaginary friend.

Pull Johnny from the wreck of an automobile. Grab Johnny, whose bike took a spill and scattered him across the track. Find Johnny at the bottom of a ravine, all blood-bone stuck-out parts and limp muscle pieces in a pile. Read Johnny palms, one at a time, and both with the same message glowing from the lines carved here and there,—a message that says No, No, No, not this one much more than a little while.

Grab Johnny's cock from his pocket and put it in our pocket for later. Use it later, dead-Johnny's Johnny.

Make more Johnnies. The world can be full of them. This world can be full of them.

What do we know from sex? Skirts and curiosity is what we know from sex. What we know about where sex comes from is that sex comes from a place that comes later than we are, but we found our way to it anyway. Miracle!

The result of the fact that God loves us!

Or if not God, well, certainly the gods love us. God may be indifferent. (Shouted from the rafters we hear, "GOD IS INDIFFERENT, BITCH!") The gods aren't indifferent. They walk around and fuck us when we're sad. Or pretty. Sorry. I meant pretty. They fuck us when we're pretty.

The fact that we're sad, too, is just a coincidence.

Back at the racetrack, the world of Johnny is ending and we're there to watch it all happen. Spring sun. Summer breeze. Fall chill. Winter silence. Everything all at once in the mind of dying Johnny and then therefore reflected in the eyes of dying Johnny and felt here inside myself. And you yourself, too.

Back at the racetrack, the other motorcycles have reappeared and are zooming by us on the track, past me kneeling on the ground, and Johnny crumpled in my arms, and you floating high above us.

Back at the track, the checkered flag has waved and a winner has been recognized. The music is swelling around us, but it's tragic minor keys in the ears of us, while maybe somewhere else triumphant major chord pomp in the ears of some other couple in some other story.

Johnny and I sit down one night and we go through the things that have happened over the last month of our relationship to see if we can find some reason for me to break his heart. It takes a while, as we have both been faithful and kept one another in our respective hearts and all that.

We search for most of the night, chain smoking and filling a white board with ideas. Brainstorming. Just throwing things out there.

Another girl you bought a soda for at the malt shop? Another girl you stopped off to help change a flat tire for one night when it was dark and things could easily be confused? An older woman who made a pass at you, like, say, the school nurse when you got in a fight over me and had to get bandages in the places where you were maybe cut?

It's a toughie. We spend all night. And then you pipe up and say we could probably just go with the wrong side of the tracks, I have money and people and Johnny doesn't, and we agree and shake hands.

And I break Johnny's heart.

If only you had piped up sooner, we could gotten to it quicker, and maybe gotten, also, a good night's sleep.

The gods of speed and recklessness are the first to bless our break-up by arranging a motorcycle race.

The gods of slippery pavement and tearful pop songs meet for the first time in many years and hammer out a friendship. (They put aside their differences! They put aside their differences!)

God is sick of tragedy and stays out of the whole mess.

I meet Johnny on the pavement. I watch him as he dies.

I circle and I circle and I circle.

You pull the needle and start it up again.

THE LONGER YOU WAIT BEFORE YOU LOOK THROUGH THE GLASS, THE FARTHER AWAY THE SHIPS WILL BE

In time, you will forget about them leaving. You will act as though the leaving never happened, and that it never tore you apart to watch them go. When they are gone, you will clean out the room in which you let them sleep, the nights they came home in time to do so. They loved to stay out late, and that was difficult for you, too, but that was not as difficult as it is going to be for as long as it takes you to forget. You had a hard time right off, and a few of us spent hours pitying you. Our hours we spent together, over some sort of Irish tea that we all enjoyed (as much as a group full of pity could enjoy), but Steven. Steven has never enjoyed tea, as far as I, or any of us, can tell. We gather together for tea and pity, but Steven never drinks from his cup. He leaves his cup on the table to cool, and we talk about how bad we all feel for whomever it is we feel bad for. A waste of tea, if you ask me, but it is not my place to confront Steven on things like this, so I don't.

You will forget, and it is important that you try and remember that. We've all of us had a chance to forget in our times, and that's what we have to offer you—the experience of forgetting. Take it from us.

The windows on our building are barred, not to keep us in, but to keep others out. So they tell us. When you look out the windows, the bars separate what you see into six frames. The sky beyond is often nothing but a haze floating over the churning water. Our building is aluminum taupe outside, walls of taupe on the inside, but all the furniture is a chocolate brown, as are the bars. But, our clothes—oh, our clothes—are whatever color we want them to be. Whatever shade in the orange family we want. Any one. Any. One. That's how the staff can tell us from the furniture.

You'll be all right. We all get passed it. We all make it through. We all forget. We all move on. We all become content. This is the day room, and this is the mess. This is the reading room, where everyone stays quiet and allows others to concentrate on their books. This is the porch, where we sit and feel the wind in our ears. This is the ocean that they made, and it stretches out for as far as we can see, but then our eyes are not what they used to be—if we're lucky. This is your bedroom, and that's the corner where you put the cots for them to sleep on.

Your time is worth more to you than you may ever know, my friend. Let's try to do something with that. Let us try to convince you of that, so you can move on. Move on, kiddo, move on.

This (here) is us on our last, last, very last legs. This (here) is where we make a final stand. This (here) is where we must learn to forget everything that isn't here in this. You now have permission to think about you and no one else except you. Savor it. Internalize the permission and pretend we didn't give it to you, but you gave it to you. Allow that to happen. Join us; and then join us in the atrium for an afternoon's contemplation of our personal pains and our personal pleasures. Let us, gathered together in the atrium, turn our gazes inward, where all the truly good stuff happens.

Screw your ungrateful kids. Screw them sideways, my dear, new friend. Screw those bastards sideways.

You are discouraged from your rooftop kite flying, as it looks to many of us as if you are trying to send out "signals." You, on our rooftop, in a light summer dress, the string gently stirring in your hand; your other hand pulling at the taught line, perpendicular to the line progressing up; your pinky acting as the intersection of a right angle, hand strung to hand, hand strung to box kite in the sky above. As attractive as we find it to watch—so sure are your lovely, lovely hands—we would all like you to stop.

Do you think you can catch them and pull them back in? Do you believe that the box kite is a baited hook, and will allow you to reel the ships back to you, returning them? So old. You're so old and set in your ways. You're nearly 23.

We remember 23, just barely. Ten years of making babies and into retirement we were taken. Into the bosom of the state we were delivered. Settle in, grandmother.

STYLES

Well—well, there were the styles to find. And, that's what there was. A style to find. Or two. Or many. And, well, we approached that, from the side, quiet-like, and well. Well, as we approached it, this style thing, as we approached it, it shrank back. And, well, it disappeared as it shrank. Into itself. Into it. Inhaled, well, is what it seemed to do. And it was, then, at that point, all style and little else. But, the style was really what we were looking for. Hunting for. Grabbing for. We needed it.

It's like, well, it's like something to hold onto. The style that we were searching for. A style is, well, it's not permanent, or edible or valuable in and of itself. The style is, it feigns the outer and enlightens the inner. Does that make sense? Have you tried a style before? It's, well, it's better than you'd expect. It's new. A very new thing.

Removing a style is easy once you get the hang of it. And you have to keep them, it's important to keep them in the nets, because if they are allowed to pull way, way in, to inhale, then all bets are, well, all bets are, are off. I saw this partisan, this young one, this, well, greenhorn type, and he was making his approach and was all ready to drop the cord around its neck, and that's when it— zip—went away. Once they're away, there's, well, there's not much to be done, I can tell you.

You can't domesticate it, not even if you try. You

can't convince any of them to come and live in your home with you. They won't go. They'll, well, they'll just make such a fuss. They kick and they spit and they—pop—are gone. And that's that. So, I know you were going to ask about that. About domestication. Don't. I've already answered your question before you had a chance to ask. Before, I'll bet, before you even had a chance to formulate it as a question, yes? Bet I did. Bet. It was floating there, but it wasn't, you know, a question yet. Yet. Beat you to it.

This style I have is brand new. It's sharp around the edges, but once you get past it to the inside, it's, well, it's softer and has a criss-cross. That strengthens it, you see. Strengthens the bonds, thread to thread. Pulses, they tend to move, well, they always seem to move across the threads just right, if that makes sense. Do you see? When I lift this one and let just a little bit dribble down? Do you? See? Do you?

No but, not mine. This one we were looking for last time. The one that inhaled and popped out of existence shrank away like a turtle-into-shell. Yeah, well, yeah. We missed it. I'm not sure what then.

There were hunters and there were founders and there was another young partisan under a hunter's tutelage when we saw just what, well, just what it was we were looking for and damned if it wasn't a *pretty* one, yes? And then this, well, this anchor began to drop, yes? This anchor we were using *gave way*. And that wasn't what we'd wanted. It's, well, it's an anchor and all of that, so when it gave way, and the founders, they began to slip and they began to *tug*, and the hunters began to call out and out, and, no. No we weren't sure then what. So, it was slipping back and back and there was a sound thrumming through the water as it happened. And as it happened we tried, we *tried* to reattach to the anchor which is, well, it doesn't happen much or often or ever if you're lucky— unattaching—so it was new, but we *scrambled* to reattach. I caught sight, then, just for a minute, yes? Can I tell you that? Can I tell you that just for one hot *second* I caught sight and, well, there wasn't much to say after that. I saw that style it had to it. I, well, if for just a minute, it really made me lose what I was *supposed* to be thinking about and I, just for a second now, I didn't do what it was I was suppose to do. That style, yes? And anchors away.

This one hunter called out and it *snapped* me back. The anchor fell but was stopped by something, a, well, a stopping thing caught it, nice and right. And that was good, yes? This partisan, though, he had other things that he was looking forward to, and no one was paying attention behind. It doesn't go so well when people get distracted. It goes badly, in fact. Bad badly. And that wonderful style just—pop—was gone. It with it. It took it wherever it is they take them. Lower, I guess. Lower and, well, quieter, yes? Here's one for you. It's coming up. There, yes? See? That one's yours if that's what you want. That one there. Not there. *There* there. There!

Don't punish it, whatever you do. It can only lead to *trouble*. Don't look away, and don't punish it. This is the net you can use. This pole will also be helpful. I can go in first, and that may make it *easier* for you. I'll shine a light on it. I'll hold your arms back. I'll stroke your arms while you grab if you think that would help. I'll put my hands on your face if that seems to make you more *comfortable*. Just say when and where and why. Okay? Well? Okay? Yes?

We all live in a yellow submarine. We hunt the waters for styles, right, during the hours of artificial sun-up to sundown, because it is dangerous at the other times. The thick sheet of ice above our ship conducts a long, flat luminescence shined from the orbiting lights.

My father, you see, my father had much more serious dreams for me than this. He didn't think our place—you remember my family's place, yes?—suggested a life like this. He didn't think much of work with the hands and the reactive brain. He didn't think much of a religious calling, you know? He did not want a son who served God. He believed, what it was was, he believed in the life of high finance, not a life in the drink.

I want you to watch out for afterthoughts. They can really mess everything up down here. They end you, you know. End you. The fangs of an afterthought, they can pull the meat from your arm in such a short amount of time. Such a short amount, you know? You've seen it happen, yes? Torn away? Afterthoughts sneak. Nothing sneaks like an afterthought. They act suddenly, yes?

BAKA IS THE NIGHT

What were this morning the whites of my eyes are this evening a mess of branching red veins. To look at them in the mirror makes me think of a negative image of the canals on the surface of the planet Mars, where I thought about going once, many years ago, but didn't think it would be right to leave my cat in the care of a neighbor for the entire three-year commitment. A week would've been reasonable. A month, perhaps, I could've gotten away with. But certainly not three years.

Mrs. Akiyama is, on average, a patient woman, but not always. I think she and Sgt. Bilko would've gotten along famously. I think she—Bilko, I mean—would've been standoffish until night fell, and then would've softened and purred her way to Mrs. Akiyama's lap. Bilko was like that with me on our very first night together. She came in through the window, having climbed the fire escape, and declared her intention to make my home her own, but would not approach me until I lay in bed. Then, it was mewl and cautiously pad to the crook of my arm, and mewl and purr, and sleep till dawn. She ran and hid under the couch when I stirred the next morning. And the next, and the next, again. It took weeks for her to trust me.

I've only learned one word of Japanese from Mrs. Akiyama. Baka, she says. Whenever something aggravates her, it's baka. Baka is the mail carrier when she doesn't bring a letter from her son in Columbus, Ohio. Baka is Mr. Naylor's little mop dog that will bark and bark throughout the afternoon. Baka are the kids downstairs who play their music too loud and way too late at night, every single weekend. Baka. Baka. Baka. Dumb. Dumb. Dumb.

A herd of tiny wild horses runs through the deep shag carpeting in my living room. It's a green and gold weave, so I bet it reminds them of a field of drying prairie grass. They make a surprising lot of noise. When they stampede from behind the sofa to below the coffee table, it's like a little thunderstorm. Sgt. Bilko runs into my bedroom every time and I comfort her however I can.

That's why I'm so very tired tonight and my eyes look as bad as they do. Sgt. Bilko and I are twisted like two layers of a cinnamon roll and she's shivering a little in the center. The damned horses. They are so small. I wonder why she won't eat them, why she doesn't give chase, capture, and bat at them. Why doesn't she toy with them, back and forth between her paws?

Mrs. Akiyama is in her apartment, awake and annoyed. She's yelling, "*Baka, baka,*" slipping between Japanese and English, saying she'll call the cops if the damn kids don't turn down that music. She says she's not afraid of them no matter how much they threaten her. She'll call the cops again and the cops will come and they'll bust the kids and they'll take their stereo this time. They told her they would. The horses are louder and a jungle has grown in the hallways. Monkeys and ugly big-beaked birds are whooping and crying and using obscene language. There's wood splintering, trees toppling in the jungle.

Mrs. Akiyama stops yelling and there's a crash.

My Martian travel agent calls once a week to ask if I've reconsidered. She thinks the trip would be good for me and says my daughter thinks so, too. When I ask about the robots we've sent up there, she changes the subject and asks if I've gone out of the apartment in the last few days. She won't talk about any of the things the robots found beyond the resort hotels and fancy golf courses of Mars.

There's a long, loud hiss in the sky and I'm pretty sure it's because the sun has sprung a leak.

When I lift open my curtains to take a look, it smarts for a second and then I see a long, cloudy trail from the sun smearing across the blue world's ceiling. "Is it safe to travel in space when the sun leaks," I ask. "Hydrogen is highly combustible."

When I go downstairs to get the mail, I notice the hallways are covered with drawings and words. "Native Mob," one says. "G-Wolf". There are little pictograms, crowns and guns and pitchforks. "Folks," one says. "Jap Bitch!"

Akiyama means "Mountains in the Autumn", but backwards. All the Japanese speak and think in reverse. That's the difference between East and West. They think, and possibly live, in reverse. I'm pretty sure, anyway. That's what I've gleaned from Mrs. Akiyama's name. I'm good with interpreting things from names. Names are magic. Names are bottomless wells of the symbols that explain the world to us.

"Carl, you really shouldn't be drinking alcohol," the travel agent told me. I have my groceries delivered and they always bring my bottles of gin along. I don't like drinking the faucet water because it comes from the lake below the building and I know the thing that swims around in there. Leviathan, it's called. Leviathan is so big and old, it scares God himself. So, I drink gin. I do not want Leviathan to get inside me, to swallow any of its infecting sperm cells.

For two nights, the horses have run through the living room and the jungle has grown in the halls. Sgt. Bilko and I have hidden deep under the blankets and I've told her don't worry. You don't need to worry. Don't be frightened. Mrs. Akiyama hasn't made a fuss: no one's *baka*. Don't be frightened, little Bilko. Tomorrow, we'll order tuna fish. Stop your shaking.

I hear Mr. Naylor and Mr. Holt and Mrs. Frey making phone calls. This time, they will come by and take away the stereo for good.

On Mars, there are vast, now-dry riverbeds, larger than any canyon that has ever scarred the Earth. And, thousands of years ago—when those carved valleys in the red sand were filled with rushing waters—the old gods held yearly festivals where they raced catamarans. They wore their khaki trousers rolled up to the calf. They drank powerful intoxicants. They fired things very much like guns in the air. I told Mrs. Akiyama about these races over tea and bean jam buns. She had come over to check up on me. Bilko watched her closely from top of a chair. Mrs. Akiyama said she had heard about those catamaran races, and we wondered what it would have been like to watch them from the shores. Mrs. Akiyama had little threads of black in her gray hair, just hear and there, and she was a tiny woman, that day. She walked slowly, drank her tea slowly.

Roger Akiyama is a very handsome Japanese man. I kind of think the Japanese are all more attractive than Westerners. I like the almond shape of their eyes a lot and I don't like it when people refer to them as "slanty." They're not. They're the shape of almonds. I read them described like that somewhere and the next time I saw Mrs. Akiyama, I noticed how apt it was as a descriptive. I said it over and over to myself as I walked away. Almond is a nice word. It's gentle, curved, and very soft. It begins with two very tall letters, but the fall in the next is cushioned by the pillowy next letters. Almond is shaped like a comfortable bed with a large headboard and posts. I tell my travel agent about the eyes and she says, Carl, that sounds racist. Eyes are eyes. I say it's a nice thing I'm saying. It's a compliment I'm saying. And she says, Compliments can be racist, too, Carl.

Roger is studying law at the University of Ohio in Columbus. Mrs. Akiyama says he has the best grades of his class. When I speak to him, he strikes me as very, very bright.

I like this Roger Akiyama. He asks me about a few nights ago and I'm not really sure what to tell him. A woman who sometimes visits me is with him and two police officers as well. We talk about how much noise there was and how very frightened my little Sgt. Bilko was. The woman gets me a glass of water from the tap. She cleans it out in the sink first, because all my glasses are dirty right now. She rinses and then wipes it down with one of the napkins I have sitting on the counter. They've pulled the curtains away and opened the window, and little Bilko is sitting on the sill smelling the afternoon air. It's a really pleasant day out today, apparently. I tell Roger I'd consider going out on a constitutional and would ask him to walk with me if it wasn't for my cat. I wouldn't want her to be lonely and frightened without me. She's the sort that would be.

I pour the water down the sink before drinking it. No one asks why and I don't feel like telling, anyway. The lady asks if I can focus for a little while longer. Roger says his mother won't be coming around anymore. This, I remind myself, is likely an example of Roger's backwards thinking.

In the other room, someone says it's not important because of DNA. Someone says someone was torn open. Torn open like a letter, I'm sure they mean. Paper ripped at a seam.

When my little Ruthie calls me on the telephone, I tell her about all the first things, all the principles and solid, brute animals that predate all the creations and all the religions and all the godly ascensions. I tell about the very, very old things, the ones who made the rules, who made the rules that all the gods of the Earth have had to follow. Your crucifix and Mrs. Akiyama's shelf of photos of her relatives—those things that you ask for attention and ask for forgiveness. They in turn must turn their minds to Leviathan, Darkness, Mathematics, Sex, the Trees. So many others. Ruthie says she's heard this before. I've told her many times and would I please, please concentrate for a minute on what she has to say. I remind her of the Tree of the Knowledge of Good and Evil. A first thing, I tell her. It liberated man and woman from the Garden, just as it had liberated the Serpent only hours before. It's not safe in that neighborhood anymore, Ruthie says. You can come live with us.

But, I like it here, and Bilko likes it here. And I won't leave her for Mars. No, I'm staying.

A new group of kids has moved in below. A noise, moving furniture and men with graceless steps comes from Mrs. Akiyama's apartment.

I will not go to Mars, no matter how many times they ask me. I will stay here with my Sgt. Bilko, and I will not leave. This is our home.

We have not heard Mrs. Akiyama yelling, which means she has found some sort of peace with our neighbors. That gives us hope.

3 WAYS I DON'T WANT TO DIE

Alan,

I've been thinking a lot about it and I've decided some things. There are some very specific ways that I don't want to die and I think that the best thing to do is for me to go ahead and enumerate them here in this letter to you because I believe that even though the universe is a dark and unjust place—the sort of place where one might find oneself on the business end of a death that one fears the most—it also has stitched into its makeup a system for prioritizing stunning novelties on those within it that are capable of that kind of thing. The universe—consciously or unconsciously, depending on your worldview—moves toward making things new and surprising. So I believe strongly that by putting these thoughts out there into the world, I am in some way inoculating myself from them. Only time will tell, I suppose.

1) I don't want to die alone in the office while I'm sitting at my desk working and fielding texts from you about when I think I am going to maybe be home for dinner or a late dinner or a very late dinner. I don't want to be alone and in the half-dark, annoyed and trying to make sense of the schedules of the many people I support. Annoyed at my phone on my desk or in my pocket when it shudders with a text from you asking when I'm going to

head home. Annoyed when it seems like you just texted me and I responded. Annoyed when I realize that it was forty minutes ago that you texted me, not five minutes ago, and it makes perfect sense you are texting me again. I don't want to die annoyed by whatever day of the week it is, which is just like every other day of the week at my job. Which is just like the first day at my job. Which is just like, I'm betting, the last day at my job. I don't want to die annoyed because there is no emotional state of less consequence than annoyance. There is no more worthless way to feel about things than to be annoyed by them. I don't want that to be the last way I feel. I'd prefer anger or even sadness. Confusion. Hopelessness. Anything but annoyance.

I don't want to die at 8:45pm in my cubicle after everyone else has gone home and the only sound is the sound of the guy from Operations whistling "Dust in the Wind" over and over and over again like he does. The one who whistles the first verse and then the chorus, and then repeats the chorus, and then does the verse, and then repeats the verse, and then does the chorus four or five more times. And never anything else. Just those two sections of the song, over and over. No bridge. No violin solo. I don't want to, say, have a brain aneurysm rupture while I'm listening to him do that. I don't want to die and start falling into my own consciousness and find myself trapped in some sort of dustbowl purgatory, my soul alone and haunting a vast, empty prairie, followed for all eternity by a high, lonely sound.

2) I don't want to die in a car accident, especially now that I have figured out how to put the car seat into the

back. And I don't think it's ever going to come out. It took me so long to figure out how to loosen the buckle of the seatbelt and feed it around the back of the car seat's base, and strap it in tight. I don't think I can remove it. I don't want to remove it. I don't want to go through that again.

Honestly, I don't want to try. I just want it to stay in there and I don't care if that means we won't be able to have a fourth person in the car ever again. I really just don't care. I still have a bruise on the top of my hand from the evening I spent trying to get the car seat in the car.

And because there isn't a baby to use the car seat yet, dying in a car accident in a car with an as-of-yet only aspirational car seat seems like one of the most intensely sad ways to die. Like one of those, "Oh, how sad. He was looking toward the future but he'll never see it come," sorts of deaths that is so popular with sentimental people. I don't want to die for the emotional catharsis of sentimental people.

I don't want to be reaching for the radio and be struck by an inattentive teenager. I don't want to feel my body in motion and have my soul push free from my body, stuck and straining until it snaps away. I don't want my soul in motion to be my eternal state, speeding away from the car forever and ever, speeding up and speeding up until I am going so fast, I'm everywhere in the universe all at once, and then I am the universe and have to feel everything that the universe feels for always, and all because someone was texting someone else that they would be there soon.

3) I don't want to die in St. Petersburg, beaten to death, standing outside an orphanage because you and I are

holding hands. I have been watching all the videos on Youtube about the people in Russia who target young gay men or gay couples, and how the police don't really do much about it. And say that's what happens: we go to Russia and we find an orphanage in, I guess, St. Petersburg—you know more about this stuff than I do because you're the one looking into it—and we're nervous and excited and in order to alleviate some of the stress we are feeling, we do what we always do. We do what lots of people do. You grab my hand. You step closer and our shoulders touch. Our arms touch. Our legs touch.

Anyone seeing that would understand the gesture. Anyone seeing that would know what the relationship between us is. Everybody knows about that way that people make contact with one another in times of stress when those people are emotionally invested in one another.

What if the wrong person sees that, and that person is with other wrong people? What if we get harassed, and then we get attacked? What if, so close to what we want, we're killed? We die? What if our hands are together, and then they are ripped apart, and we spin away and spin away outward and we never see each other again? Or just experience each other again? All because we held hands?

I don't want to die like that.

Love,
Me

UNDERLINGS: A REBUKE

It was underlings. All of them, everywhere, underlings. I took me an issue or two.

But then what good was it? None. None at all good.

That one there is ceremonial green. This one here is matrimonial blue.

Underlings. The fuckers. Under-fucking-lings.

And I argued. I argued an argue that it seemed to me made a whole hell of a lot of better sense than all that that they were tossing off.

Tossing out into the air.

Underlings, all of them.

"Underlings, all of you," I said loud. That one over there in obscene, obscene red.

I did this all because what it is that I am is a man. And I burned that building to the very ground it was there standing on.

AMERICANS AFTER AMERICA

And so there came a day when, as one, the Americans arrived at a thought. It was suddenly clear and obvious and irrefutable: America—their beloved, vast, well-developed country—was, in fact, not really theirs. They had taken it—with boats, with muskets, with blankets soaked in disease, with numbers. (Oh, so many numbers.) And the full meaning of that—of them having taken their country—hit them all at once. The magnitude of it. The consequences of it. The possibility that their was really a lot of injustice in it.

And arriving together at that thought, the Americans did what Americans were so famous the world over for doing. Because the Americans were—at bottom—a just people, because the Americans were—at heart—a good people, and because the Americans were—in a pinch—a generous people, the Americans decided that, after all the years of American history (which they had acquired in first a handful and then a large pile of states united together for the purpose of acquiring a history) that it was time they maybe went ahead and left those states to the original owners, to let them take it back over, to let them maybe come up with a new government, to let them maybe come up with a new flag, to let them decide if they wanted to, say, keep the border configurations as is, or perhaps come up with a whole new setup or whatever.

Because, really, whatever. It was going to be their country again. The Americans thought it gauche to make suggestions on their way out. (Because the Americans are, we all know, a humble people, uninterested in meddling in the affairs of others.)

It was, as I said, quite sudden. There they were, these Americans, watching televised football or watching televised poker or checking the internet to see about their fantasy football teams or playing online poker, and then they had their epiphany. "We should maybe go," they said to one another. They had that tone where what they said was both a statement and a question. Like, they asked a question but ended it in a period.

"Should we maybe go."

And yes, they all agreed. They should probably go. And they should probably not make a big deal out of it, too, because Americans are—you might remember or you might have been told—not into making a big thing out of things. They like to be subtle. They don't care for drama. Americans are inconspicuous.

The Americans packed up travel bags. Some packed heavy. Some packed light. Americans traveled in so many different ways. The Americans left behind most of what they had acquired over the years and years they had spent living in America—a place wherein the acquisition of things was made easy in a way that it was the envy of the rest of the world, which sometimes seemed to the non-Americans to be tacky. But, in fact, the truth about the Americans and their will to acquire is more complicated than it seems when only the surface of the American character is analyzed. Unpack the American zest for the gathering of and subsequent use of or storing of things, and one finds that hidden within it, buried in the recesses of the American psyche, the seeds of the American expatriation. Always there within was the leaving. Implicit in its founding, the Americans looked toward their great sovereign state's dissolution—like every birth announcement carries in it, subtextually, the coming obituary—and the Americans implanted in their character an acquisitiveness not because they lacked tact, but because they desired to leave a lot of things behind for the original owners of the land they had called America. Because that is what they did. They left almost all of it behind. In their houses. At their offices. In the safety deposit boxes with the keys and accompanying numbers and locations. With the directions to the hidden safes and lock combinations. The Americans left all this out on kitchen tables. With notes. Notes that said:

"Hey, sorry about all this. You can keep the stuff, if you want. Because, I mean, our bad and all that."

Spiritually speaking, the Americans were made stronger by the sudden loss of so much acquired consumable material. Or, the sudden casting off of said. Walking away from all the things weighing them down—please forgive the cliché—made a much lighter people of them.

So, small bags packed, a map or two, a guidebook, and with all the American airlines and ocean liner owners and rail services agreeing to make final gratis runs out of the country to far-flung destinations, the Americans, in the dead of night, left. So the story goes, they sang as they set out for the world. So the story goes, the National Anthem was neglected because a consensus could not be reached on all the lyrics—a second verse? A third? A fourth? Did anyone really know them?—and no American could adequately deal with the vocal range needed to properly sing a song that, we don't hesitate to point out, had been chosen specifically for the ambition of its melody. (Because the Americans were an ambitious people.)

Not a one could hit the notes. Not a single American. And because the Americans were a realistic people, they did not try. They choose, instead, the song that both spoke to the American character and that fit the American pitch limits. So the story goes, they sang Take Me Out to the Ballgame.

Here's what the Americans learned when they left America and entered the world as Americans without America:

—Americans learned new languages. Attached as they had been for so many years to the English language, the one they had borrowed from, well, the English, the Americans learned that they needed to—in certain places, anyway—become familiar in rudimentary or comprehensive ways with new languages—the languages of the world. (The ones, they were happy to admit, that had so flummoxed them when they were still in America.) So they did what they needed. In their own inimitable American style, the Americans went online and bought audio files of recorded language instruction. For long months, the Americans walked the streets of their new homes— in Europe, in Asia, in Africa, in Australia—earbuds inserted deep in their ears, sheepish, apologetic looks on their faces when they accidentally stepped out into traffic or bumped into a stranger and were unable to apologize in the local language, and the Americans learned. As Americans do. Americans learn. They walked around with their iPods or other mp3 playing devices held in their hands and they listened and they mumbled to themselves with just a little self-consciousness. "Petit dejeuner," they said. "Watashi wa John Smith desu," they said. It should be noted, though, that no matter how hard they tried, Americans never truly lost their accent, no matter what language they used to replace English.

And over time, English itself began to loose its global ubiquity. The language that had become the language of international business—because of American corporate power—was allowed to isolate itself once again to the obscurity of the British Isles and the Australian continent. And in its place, Chinese took over as the dominant language of international conference calls and meant-to-impress client dinners.

—The Americans learned the great pleasure of being outside. At first, the Americans approached their new surroundings like tourists. They had so many new places to discover, so many old buildings to stare at and, in groups, to comment on the ages of to one another. (America, for all its history, was such a young country. Its buildings were all so young. to be around so many old buildings was, in the words of many an American, "Totally GD charming. Can you believe how charming it all is? Look how old!") So, the Americans approached their new homes in touristy sorts of ways, in touristy sorts of outfits, with touristy kinds of attention. Before the Americans found themselves settling into whatever lives they were going to make for themselves in their new homes, the Americans sight-saw. And with all this time outside, walking around, the Americans began to find that they enjoyed the sun. They enjoyed the physical activity. They enjoyed getting a little tan below the sleeves of their shirts, and they enjoyed wearing visors. They enjoyed cafes, and they enjoyed decks overlooking the streets, and they enjoyed the random attention of cats and dogs that had made the streets their homes. They enjoyed strolling.

The Americans, after learning a great affection for being in the out-of-doors, eventually found work in the out-of-doors. Many had left office jobs in America, had left cubicles and desks and hands-free headsets for multi-lined phones, but in the world, the Americans gravitated to work that involved the use of their hands, and a ceiling not of square, replaceable panels, but of sky. Light not from buzzing florescent bulbs, but from the big, yellow sun.

—The Americans learned to eat butter. The Americans learned to ride public transport to and from work. The Americans learned how to have affairs, and be aware of friends having affairs, without telling anyone about it, to cultivate tact and avoid gossip. The Americans learned to take longer vacations. The Americans learned to write letters to one another, actual letters that they put in envelopes and mailed to the friends they'd had back when they were Americans in America. The Americans learned to read books, and to find a way to allow themselves the free time to read books. The Americans learned how to listen to the stories older people told, and learned to remember them, and learned to take lessons that they could apply to their lives from them. The Americans learned to cry when they were happy. The Americans learned to laugh off rotten luck. The Americans learned—truly, truly learned—how to spot and really appreciate irony.

The world did not immediately accept the Americans. They were Americans after all. They had a reputation. Not a bad reputation, necessarily. Not a good reputation, either. They simply had a reputation. They had a reputation for being Americans. And the world remembered what they had been like when they were Americans with an America. Some remembered it when the Americans had invaded them, and it was not a happy memory. Some remembered a time when they had hoped the Americans would invade them, and it was also not a happy memory. Some remembered aid to dictators. Some remembered the lack of aid after a natural disaster. Some simply remembered that time when the American basketball player dunked on one of their own during the Olympics, and the way he had grabbed his crotch, and let out a loud howl, and they remembered not really thinking that behavior was very sporting.

These new Americans—these Americans without an America—remembered those things, too. Not always in the same ways, sure. But they remembered them. And they made a humble face. And they held up their hands. And they said, "Sorry about that. But, hey, here we are. Mind if we move in next door? We keep our lawns neat and we love to invite neighbors over for barbecues and such."

And they did not blend in, the Americans. And they

attempted to blend in. They really did. But they never really could. First generation. Second generation. Third generation. They spoke their new languages as Americans—with their flat, American accents. They wore their new clothes as Americans, with a tightness at the collar and a looseness at the waist. They ate as Americans, drank as Americans. Made friends as Americans. Worked as Americans. There was some essential nature to them, some aura around them, something—perhaps just a particular way they walked—that continued for a long time to mark them as Americans. And this, for a time, made the world uncomfortable. Just a little.

But, really, it didn't bother the Americans. They did not feel as if they needed to be ashamed of their American-ness. They enjoyed it. And because the Americans had an enthusiasm about themselves as Americans, eventually that enthusiasm infected the people of their new homes. It infected the world.

The world learned from the Americans. More than anything else, the world learned a happy kind of urgency. As the Americans learned to slow down, the world learned to speed up, and somewhere in this came a kind of cohesion. As the world ingested the American character, and as the Americans allowed themselves to be consumed by the world community, the American-ness became a kind of nutrient. This American-ness flowed in a great planetary bloodstream and it fed and it fed and it fed the world. So, for a time, the world had this rhythm to it. This pulse. This charge. It was exciting, the world moving ahead, maybe not paying as much attention to its heading and its destination. Just moving, and moving so fast that half the history that was happening didn't even get written down. Because who had time to write anything down? Because everything just wants to move.

Eventually the Americans—without their America, within the world—melted away. Became history. Assimilated fully. Generations had passed and the accent disappeared, and the clothes began to fit right. And the once-Americans became not Americans without America, but Russians in Russia. And Australians in Australia. And Indians in India. And Germans in Germany. And some even became French.

But a bit of the charge is still here. The world still pulses a little from the infusion of Americans it got all those years ago. And sometimes you'll meet a person, and you'll talk to that person, and you'll get to know that person, and get to like that person, and you'll notice within that person a quality. And you notice it but you don't say anything. And they notice you noticing it, and they don't say anything, either. Because Americans never liked to make a big deal out of things.

THE IN-BETWEENS

We're here—that sweetheart Donna D and I—stuck in the In-Betweens and the darn thing only just started. So it must be Monday. We're floating near the ceiling of the cave, the slick back rocks so close we can strain and touch them with our noses. The water was flooding into the cave through a spout in the rocks above, but it's stopped its gushing. A trickle still filters in, and a drip echoes through the tiny space left between the water's surface and the rock canopy above. We're safe in the In-Betweens, dog-paddling or floating on our backs, drifting in the settling waters.

We wait out our first evening without a word to each other, take the quiet as an opportunity to relax from all the excitement. Recent events, the ones that left us together in the bottom of this cave at Black Rock Gulch, have been exhausting, and the In-Betweens is a welcome rest. We even manage a few hours of uninterrupted sleep—no blaring Ranger Signal, no assaults on any secret mountain headquarters, no unexpected explosions, kidnappings, assassination attempts on U.S. Senators, poachers, or foreign invaders. Just peace, a quiet drifting in and out of consciousness.

Donna D, she asks, "Sagebrush Bobby, what did y'all dream last night?"

I tell her about having one of recurring library dreams. In last night's, I saw myself from a few feet above, sitting at a wooden table with a pile of books and a stack of blank note cards. I was searching through the index of each book, looking for something. I ran my index finger down, stopped on a line, found a page number, searched the text of the book, found a page, searched the paragraphs, found a passage, and made notes on a note card. The dream was long—lingering and slow. I filled dozens of note cards before I woke up.

"What did you dream about, sweetheart Donna D?" I ask.

"Sky Screamin' Ranger Rex," she answers. Every time she's stuck in the In-Betweens, she dreams of the man who will rescue her come In-Betweens' end. She sees his shining badge and six-shooters, his strong chin and black eye mask, his wingpack. She hears him singing his favorite song, the one about the lonesome Wyoming plains that raised him, accompanied by the other Rangers—Injun Mike, Shep, Lyle, and me. He gently strums the strings of his guitar, and he never uses a pick. He never uses his nails. He plays with the soft tips of his fingers: index and middle and thumb.

"Who else," I say, and I laugh, and I sigh, and the sounds all leave me and commingle in the air. "Sky Screamin' Ranger Rex. Our hero."

"Whatcha think he's doing right now?" she asks.

"I don't know," I say. But I'm lying to Donna D. Many's the time I've been stuck in the In-Betweens with Rex, and I know exactly what he's doing.

"He doesn't talk about it with me," she says. "He doesn't tell me what he does."

"No one talks about the In-Betweens except when they're in them, sweetheart Donna D," I answer. "It's just not done."

Tuesday, we do it against the cave wall. She's thinking of Rex, digging her fingers into the rock and not making a sound. We don't even talk about it first; she just gestures and hikes up her skirt.

Tuesday. This is the day Rex picks fights with everyone around him, be they bank robber or posse member. The other Rangers all do their level best to ignore him. He gets antsy, climbing up and down the walls and pacing and sipping from the flask he hides in his boot. He's knocked me senseless on a Tuesday in the In-Betweens on many an occasion, only to apologize come Wednesday, his day of reparations.

Donna D asks me, "Sagebrush Bobby, does he think about me when we're stuck in the In-Betweens? Does he fret for me?"

"He thinks about nothing but you, Donna D," I lie. "It gets so the rest of us have to ask him for a song or a story every couple of hours just to keep his mind off you and the danger you are likely in."

Donna D drops into the water when I tell her this, and doesn't come up for hours. She doesn't want me to see the tears on her face as she cries for her Ranger Rex.

Nobody dies in the In-Betweens, so she can stay down there as long as she wants without needing to come up for air.

Last night I dreamt I was an entomologist studying a brand-new type of bumblebee. Instead of yellow and black, this one was red and black. It had the most even temperament you could imagine, and it could be trained to come when you call. I had a hive of them and taught them to do all sorts of tricks you never see the bees do, like fly in a V formation and buzz at different speeds to make a sound like the way a barbershop quartet hums in harmony when they tune up their voices to sing.

I tell Donna D all about it, but she sinks down again as I'm talking and sits on the cave floor. She doesn't come up for the rest of the day.

Sky Screamin' Ranger Rex is a mess on Wednesdays, calling for whiskey and company. He stares straight ahead sometimes, like at nothing in particular. He cries a lot, apologizes, and the Rangers have all learned to let him do it and pretend it isn't happening. It only seems fair as many times as he's saved the lot of us, over and over and over. I'm a little less patient, but only because I'm rarely outside Sky Screamin' Ranger Ranch. Mostly I spend my time in the kitchen making stews of one type or another.

I get a lot of pleasure out of cooking for the boys. I don't know why. We don't have to eat in the In-Betweens, but I cook anyway. I like a good, solid knife moving through meat and vegetables. I like the way liquids stir and colors blend. I like steam floating up. I like feeding the Rangers.

Injun Mike, son of frontier folk killed on their way west, raised by the Crow Nation. Shep, the world's only talking—and singing!—dog, the result of some godforsaken science experiment with voodoo magic and brainwave enhancement through radioactivity. Young Master Lyle, the real living heir to the throne of Willonia Proper in the great, old, distant continent of Europe. The boys like to have their jokes with me, old Sagebrush Bobby. Donna D, she grabs the sombrero off my head, puts it on, and tells me not to, "pay them boys no mind." She's oh-so-gentle with the feelings of all of us, but only has real eyes for Rex.

Thursday I have my way with Donna D again, but this time she's stays underwater through it. Nary a bubble.

Then she tells me about the last time she was saved by Sky Screamin' Ranger Rex, how he swooped in just as a Martian commando was about to execute her, and how Ranger Rex brought her up into the sky. It was only for a few moments, but they were the most important few moments of her life. "He has these real solid forearms," she says.

We hold on to one another for the rest of the day, under and on top of the water. We're starting to get a little batty but you learn to savor the In-Betweens for the meditation time it gives you. And a fidgety leg can be comforted by a few laps around the cave.

Once Injun Mike smoked a cigarette with me behind the bunkhouse—we know it's best not to around Ranger Rex—and he asked why in the In-Betweens he feels so full while Rex and Donna D seem so empty, and the rest of the time it's just the opposite. I told him I had no earthly idea, but I knew exactly what he meant.

On Friday, a big damned hole opens up in my heart and I ask Donna D if she—with her sad, hollow eyes—could ever learn to see and old cowboy like Sagebrush Bobby. If she—with her empty, tortured heart—could ever learn to love an old cowboy like Sagebrush Bobby. Even a fraction of how much she loves her Sky Screamin' Ranger Rex. But I know she won't ever, ever answer.

"That's the Trap gotcha," young Master Lyle says. "The Trap," he calls it. More often than not, it's him stuck in the In-Betweens with the sweetheart Donna D, and the Trap always gets him on Friday. Snaps its jaws on his young boy's heart.

And on Friday, it's snaps its jaws on this old man's heart. Me and the boys, we're just as tragic as she is.

So Saturday I mostly yell at her, but I go underwater to do it so she doesn't have to hear a single, mean-spirited word of it. It's not her fault, I tell myself. It's not her fault and if I want to holler, I can do so at the bottom of the flooded cave. And I can just be there surrounded by water as ornery as I want to be. And that doesn't have a single thing to do with poor, sad Donna D floating above. She knows the In-Betweens is about to end. She's combing out her hair. She's pinching her cheeks to give them a blush. She's tending to herself.

And on Saturday it is clear to me that that big damned hole has been there for a long while, but it will go away come morning. Next In-Betweens, I expect that it won't be me stuck with sweetheart Donna D and I will forget all about it. That trap won't have a chance to get me again.

Sunday arrives and the water begins pouring in again. It looks like the end, this time, for the sweetheart Donna D and old Sagebrush Bobby, but that's when the dynamite blows. That's when the one and only Sky Screamin' Ranger Rex comes barreling in through the hole he's dynamited in the side of our rock prison, and he scoops us up by the back of our shirts and carries us out of the cave. And he sits us down in the dirt. She is just clinging to consciousness when Sky Screamin' Ranger Rex gathers Donna D up in his arms and plants a healing kiss on her sweet forehead. He leans her back into me, and he jumps to the sky, off into the yonder he flies to a thorny, unbelievable airship, guns in hands, wingpack flapping him on to save the world once more.

ISHPEMING

Ishpeming straddles Lake Superior to Marathon, reaches into the water, pulls out a clump of frozen hotdogs, breaks them apart one by one, rolls them between its fingers, heats them on the thigh of its corduroy pants, and throws them into the sky. Comets they thereup become. Ishpeming laughs like a frog.

In its lungs, cancer grows like educational sponge dinosaurs. In its brain, cancer grows like soap bubbles under a flowing faucet. In its eyes, cataracts are solidifying.

Ishpeming teases the lanes of the roads apart with his fingernail. He grasps and gives a hard tug. Cars fly off into Minnesota. The sparrows in his ears are pissing Ishpeming off.

Lodie is a sniper, and kills cities for a living. She is on a raft in Lake Michigan. When she sees Ishpeming, Lodie pulls the rifle from her back.

The bullets are filled with mercury and shaped like little drill bits. And spin like little drill bits.

Lodie steadies the boat by steadying her breathing and then steadying the water around the boat. She dips a finger in the water, and it stops all it's God damned roiling.

The shot hits Ish's temple, and it burrows in. The mercury injects, hits the blood stream, runs around looking for the heart. When the mercury finds the heart, it coats the sides and dissolves the valves between the chambers. This leaves Ishpeming royally fucked.

Lodie turns away, and does not see the city fall.

Ishpeming falls. The ground shakes and then the ground stops shaking.

Someone opens up a bottle and pours malt liquor on Ishpeming's feet. That same someone walks for a long time in order to pour malt liquor out near each of Ishpeming's hands. The bottle is empty at the final thumb and someone is unable to take a memorial drink.

God, who lives in the sky, ignores the entire situation, instead concentrating on a new project. He has started a band with some friends, and is on the phone trying to hustle up a gig or two in the next couple of months. The band has been getting pretty good lately, and has been practicing twice a week. God doesn't think much of his singing voice, but the other members of the band are pretty keen on it. It's a good time for God.

The corpse of Ishpeming does not stink as it rots to pieces. The rot is not so much organic as it is mechanical. It is, like, entropy.

Or something.

The comets, still zipping around the heavens, tears through God's drummer's neck. The drummer dies. Blood is everywhere in God's garage.

Outraged by the death of his drummer (the best of all the drummers who called God after seeing his flyer on a light pole), God destroys the universe.

WE GOT LOST ALONG THE WAY

A novelette

Jenny made a hash of it and totally got us kicked out of the ashram. Guru Jermaine was quite the little girl about the whole thing, pointing and yelling, shaking and spitting, sputtering and grabbing, pulling and pointing us to the door. And all this seemingly without mindfulness. He was spun quite a ways out from his calm, deliberate center. Guru Nancy, bless her, was mostly cool, but try as she did, she couldn't wake Jermaine to his present moment, so she stood behind him and gave us a little finger wave as we were escorted out the door.

I probably shouldn't have had sex with Guru Nancy. I mean, an argument against could certainly be made. Hindsight.

Out we went. Out the door, me looking back a little bitty bit longingly and Jenny without a care about any of it, lighting up a cigarette and dropping the matchpack—a little red and blue illustration of the ashram there on its cover—dropping it behind her like a teenager being really teenaged about things.

Jenny was settled in my hand, but after us out the door, she jumped down to the stone path and was a leaf blowing along it. I looked down and tried to give her a smile to show her that, all things in perspective, I was okay with the direction we were going, and the way it was us moving away from the ashram, much as I had loved our time in it, what with the chanting, the rice dishes, and the loose-fitting clothing and all. But we had tried so many things. And the ashram was just the most recent. That's what I was thinking, looking down at Jenny-leaf until I walked past Jenny-leaf, and Jenny (abandoning leaf) kited up into the sky and decided to become a big white cloud. A big friendly cloud that would never threaten anyone with rain. That would be Jenny for a bit.

Jenny was inclined to be many things. Sometimes big. Sometimes small. It was always hard to say where she would go and what she would be next. I never quite got a handle on it, never sussed a pattern. Always, though, she found her home in something beautiful. That I knew. I was glad to be her companion. She was full of ideas and always gave them to me freely.

I was saying: We had tried so many things over the years. Things to make us better. We had tried therapy. We had tried to be vegan. We had tried working for a while as one of those people who you walk by on the street and they stop you to tell you that if you only spare them a minute or two, you can become a soldier in the war on hunger or intolerance or some other odious thing that deserved to have a war waged upon it. We had tried yoga. We had tried a silent meditation retreat where Jenny would not even for one second shut up, and where I tried to tune her out as best as I could, and also where, when I spent any time thinking about my father or my mother, I cried. We had tried drugs. (So many drugs of so many kinds with so many interesting effects.) We had tried to reach out to our human potential—which we were led to understand was hiding in the nebulous vapors of our semi-conscious mind—and we looked to grasp it through the power of positive thinking, or through the amazing success that packs itself into the word "yes," or in the interconnectivity of a roomful of people like us just screaming and screaming and not stopping until we had no voices left. We had tried having lots of sex with lots of strangers of whatever gender those strangers happened to be identified by, wherever they swam in the fluid of gender. We were there and we were into it. We had tried the wonderful togetherness and all-over world love found at the bottom of bottles and bottles of beers and of boozes. We had tried stealing things from big box stores to get from that act of rebellion some tiny satisfaction. (So many, many things. Just stealing them. Sometimes selling them. Sometimes keeping them.) We had tried finding an ad hoc family on the streets or on the internet in chat rooms. We had tried reconnecting with our racial and geographical heritage. We had tried Marxism and we had tried Libertarianism. We had tried a religion founded by a sociopath with a grudge and a sailor's hat.

We felt like we had tried everything. And then the ashram. And then, ejected like a sour cherry pit from the mouth-door of the ashram, we were not sure what was left to try. But we knew we'd look and look and something would come up. Someday. Something would help. Something was bound to help. Jenny kept saying we should look. And I always listened to Jenny. Because then I didn't have to listen to me.

So we went north, my Jenny and me, hitchhiking. (We had tried to discover ourselves hitchhiking the American Road once. We had discovered only hunger and violence and depravity. We had discovered the outer limits of the kinds of behavior we were willing to engage in to keep safe and warm for a night in the backseat of a vehicle.) We went truck to truck to car to truck until we made it up to Washington state. We made it and we found a nice motel. We got a room—we were flush at the time and could afford such things—and went in and we took a nap. We woke up and we turned on the TV. We felt a tremor and we watched the TV news and saw California—our home, our state—fall into the ocean.

Just like that. Rumble, rumble. Snap. Crash. Water everywhere. Gone. Our home, California. Into the ocean, taking every living person of California with it. Taking every dead and buried person with it, too. Taking all the Californians away from the country forever and for good. Taking away the pets and the celebrIties and the personal trainers. Tossing into the water all the expensive restaurants and all the hybrid cars. Drowning for good and forever all the Democrats and all the seeing eye dogs and even every squirrel. Every squirrel in California. (I don't know why I think about them. Sad, I guess. Squirrels.) It was there, on the TV. The drowning deaths of the dreamy, sunny, strange, and lovely state of California and everyone in it and everyone of it. Except for a couple of us who were away at the time and saved from drowning by chance. Everyone else gone. An earthquake hit and California fell into the ocean, just like everyone joked would happen, but everyone agreed would never happen. It happened.

What a fucked up day that was.

As to whether or not the Americans were going to miss California, there was never really any consensus amongst the people. It was such a large state. It was such a difficult one to hate, what with the natural beauty and the surfing and the Hollywood. It was such a difficult one to love, what with the people and the organic food and the Hollywood.

But, still, a piece of our landmass was gone. A people were gone. A tragedy had occurred, and Americans love a tragedy. Americans love a mourning period. Americans love a good empty gesture. Americans love ham-fisting a symbolic act, being really obvious about it, and also trying to find some way to televise their brave response to grief, if possible. So all those newly coastal areas, all those states that once were penned in, kept away from the long, blue-green Pacific, all those states that had quietly dreamed of themselves as owners of a beachfront, all those states that looked west to California and said, "If I had the beach, I'd do it different. I'd really take advantage of that area, not like those Californians who muscle it up with muscle-y beaches or give it to the gay people who want to live on hills, or allow a class of blonded, tan-skinned oddballs to make bums of themselves on my sand,"—all those states that now were gifted with beaches in the demise of the beachiest of states felt grouchily obligated to make their beaches just like the ones we'd lost. For consistencies sake. For the tragedy. So the world could see the Americans mourn properly for the thing they'd lost, they rebuilt it exactly as they thought it was. They—oh so pissily—remade their westernmost sides in the image of California.

Not by government decree. No one forced them to do it. The people at the edges of these newly coastal states just up and did it. They thought that's what was expected of them, so they became a memorial for their lost countrymen and countrywomen.

Such resentment! Such a fuss! Such hard work trying to remember what it had been like, that state of California!

Because no one had kept good records. No one had really paid enough attention to all the things going on out west in the state of California. And all the experts on the history and the geography of the state, so deep within the sea and unable to assist. So drowned, and lungs and voices stoppered with water, and silent. The manuscripts of their books lost. The printed copies sent back to publishers and pulped so many years ago because of disinterest in the subject from all but other Californians right up to the moment when there was no more California and there were no more Californians. (And even still, everyone knows a Californian had no time to read. Why even publish so many sure-to-be unread books?) No one with a professional title to consult. No one on speed dial to field questions. Just inattentive politicians from the other 49 states and their lacking-utterly-in-imagination builders and contractors and landscapers and architects and planners to do all the work and make all the choices. Just them rebuilding California like that proverbial room full of blind men feeling up that elephant then rebuilding the elephant out of smaller and more resentful and more conservative animals.

And so when it was, in a manner, rebuilt, it was so not really like the state that had been lost.

A handful of us really, really remembered. As I said, mostly no more Californians, but a tiny few. Only a handful of Californians were, by some dumb luck, away from our home when our home shook and shuddered and cracked off and went bye bye.

But shout as much as we did, we never got through to the planners of this plan to rebuild the beachfront. Never got a voice heard by committee or council. Try as we might, we bona fide Californians were unable to slow the forward momentum of the California coast rebuild and add fact to conjecture, truth to vague percolating memory, reality to the flat-out made-up fantasyland dream coast that was plotted out and placed there to replace the there that was not ever really there. We weren't listened to. We were coddled and pitied and ignored.

And also, at least in my case, there were all these drugs to do instead of shouting. To keep the difficult feelings away. The ones brought on by the destruction of one's beloved home state. And then the ones brought on by the weird rebuilding of one's beloved home state in states that did not really feel like home. All of those difficult feelings, and all of those drugs—returned to even though they hadn't helped at any other point when they were used to try to help—back again, quieting me. And Jenny, who, honestly, seemed unphased.

This non-California California. Look at it now. We ask you. This many palm trees? This many ferris wheels? This many shirtless men on rollerblades holding signs offering to embrace passersby without recompense? This many hemp bracelets? This many men to paint pot leaves on the shiny and innocent faces of children on vacation? This many vans? You thought we all drove vintage and muraled vans—space scenes and "killer waves" and, God almighty, unicorns? This many chilled-out dogs wearing sunglasses trained to high-five strangers? Shaved ice with watermelon in a paper cone that says, "Hang Ten" available everywhere?

This is who you thought we were? This is all you remembered of us? All that time you spent with us right there to the left of you, and given a chance to bring us back after we are taken from you, and this is what you come up with? This place? This theme park? No serious work being done? No people of substance? Nothing but sand and costumes?

Seriously? Fuck you, dudes.

§

So one day I found myself on your beach. (It's not my beach. It's not, as much as you insist it is, my California coast. It is Arizona. I know from Arizona. This is Arizona. Look around. Shut up.) Jenny was a sharpish pebble riding all pokey in my shoe and having a conversation with the bottom of my foot about the things the brain part of me did that did not make her very satisfied with all the things the brain part of me did to try to satisfy her. I was doing my very level best to stay out of the conversation, as I was convinced it mostly just concerned Jenny and my brain stem, not my brain proper. And I was not going to lower myself to her level, pun intended. Pun very much intended.

The fight was clanging on and clanging on. I saw a tall, plastic palm tree—some of these plastic trees were planted as place-holders but were never replaced by the real deal as the post-California years went by, you lazy-asses—and decided to avail myself of its sun-sheltering properties. I had not washed in days, and had not eaten in days—had only in the last hour drunk liquor given to me by a stranger in front of a liquor store when I informed said stranger I was a Californian. A real one. An actual, in the physical flesh former resident of the now-gone paradise that America had recreated and this man was now visiting? Or a citizen of? Did he want some authentic California stories? Did he want to tell his friends he met one of the real live, rare-as-fuck Californians? Did he want to study me so that his being-there-and-living-in-California life would have some real, real authenticity through his aping of my mannerisms or patterns of speech, maybe, because of how awesome and popular authenticity is? Here I was. Just a pint of bourbon away from me assisting the shit out of him and his. That's all. What a deal.

He was dubious, but I told him briefly about wine country in a way only a Californian could—in the kind of visceral detail only a real California could construct from their memories of the actual place and not some television representation, some four-part PBS kind of skimmed televisual mock-up version—and soon he was convinced enough to step into the liquor store, purchase a bottle, return to me, hand it over, thank me for my citizenship, apologize for the utter terribleness of natural disasters—that California-into-the-ocean one in particular and all the general ones in general because, Hell, what the Hell? tut at my lowly state, pat me on my grimy shoulder, turn away and leave me to my midday beach boozing.

"Poor sad man," he said. "So full of the wisdom of your people. So inconsolable in your tremendous grief. I give now to you this tiny gift of quiet, personal, liquid forgetting. Do not share it but keep it all for yourself because you deserve it more than others. And I have in my heart hope it will seem as bottomless as possible for you. May it fill today and may one of my fellow Americans and newly minted Memorial Californians help you out with a replacement bottle tomorrow. This I do pray."

That's what he said to me, handing me the booze and walking off. That is an exact, direct-ass quote, not even a smidge embellished. So, given said commanding oration—how lovely is the oration of people in these days of ours—this admonishment to drink lots and alone, that is what I went off to do.

But the tree is where I was headed, to get away from the sun, made seemingly brighter and more penetratingly awful by the bourbon that had sensitized the fuck out of my eyes. Them half closed and the dinny argument still in my foot, and the general motor-skills-poor state of my intoxicated body caused a less than beeline-like walk plastic treeward, and a less-than-attentive-to-my-surroundings-and-the-people-peopling-my-surroundings way of making my way there. That is to say, I spaced and bumped into some dude.

A dude had buried himself in the shallow sand of the makeshift beach, but even with him obvious there, and humming some melody to boot, I managed to miss him in my mind and eyes and hit him with my feet. I tripped well and truly over him and fell into the sand near him like the lower bar on a human L there on the beach waiting for a mess of humanity to arrive to add the O and the S and the E and the R and the final S to our self-describing, on-the-ground word formation. Us the world's saddest cheerleaders. But drunk and less gutted by the sad because.

"Ho-ly," he says.

"Sorry," I says, my face still mostly buried in the sand, and the puff of the apology's air disturbing a bit of it and shooting some of said into my half-open eyes, adding a scratchy element to their already light-beaten pain therein.

"Child, watch out where you are walking. You nearly hurt a real-life Californian."

"I certainly did," I says. "I nearly twisted up my very ankle."

"I meant me," he says.

"And I meant me," I says back.

I sat up and looked him over side to side and up and down. Older black man with gray hair up top and encircling his mouth. "A real, true Californian man?" I asked.

"I am indeed, son. Dr. Reed Rialto Rose. Scholar and maker of soap. Teacher and preacher of a new God's religion."

I told him my name but did not even a little, of course, hint at the presence of Jenny even though she was right there making reminding sorts of coughing noises, thinking maybe today and to this doctor would be the opportunity for me to, for the very first time, introduce her to another living soul. She's a hopeful type. I let that opportunity pass and did not feel even a bit bad about it.

"A good name, yours," said Dr. Reed Rialto Rose. "And good, too, the bottle hanging low there in your waistband. Are you, dear man, the sharing sort?"

"I am not," I said, "on any other day. Today, I feel a new leaf turning over in the tree of my brain, though."

I handed to him my quite-lighter-than-it-had-begun bottle, and pondered aloud: "Is that right? When you turn over a new leaf, is it still on the tree—and does a tree sprout from your brain? Has the brain-sprout leaf fallen to the ground, and you are checking for it to see which side is up?"

"I am certain it is a page in a book you turn when a new leaf has been turned over," he said.

"A 'page' is a 'leaf,'" I said with no little excitement. "Of course. That phrase looks so different to me, now, in my mind. It used to look one way, but what you've pointed out to me has made it change and made my original way of seeing it seem absurd. It looks so different."

"Don't it, though," he said. And drank. And drank.

The doctor had changed the way I saw something. As he would do again and again.

§

We spent the day at the beach swimming and imbibing and getting acquainted in the sunshine, which eventually felt less oppressive on my eyes as the booze dimmed the shit out of them. Jenny, quick to forget I had forgotten to introduce her yet again, enjoyed her day, choosing to spend it being the loosening elastic waistband of my once recognizably name brand boxer briefs and stopgap swim trunks, and a seagull feather I had threaded into my hair, which in those days I was wearing long and difficult. Jenny does not herself much swim, but was content to ride along with me, as I churned my hands and feet about and floated in the water for hours, the good Dr. Reed Rialto Rose shouting from the beach that I appeared blessed with a remarkable buoyancy and would make, if someday I so chose to give up my current life of leisure and work avoidance, a very excellent sailing man.

"Perhaps you could take a job on a tall ship," he said.

"They still have those. The wooden ones."

He suggested I get the pig and the cock tattooed on my calves, in the style of the sailor, to guarantee my safety should my boat sink into the icy ocean. I could get swallows and bluebirds to celebrate my arrivals home and back to my loved one. Get just all birded the fuck up, tattoo-wise. Be like a tree in a zoo aviary. Did I like to work with my hands and would I consider being a sailor? Did I have and would I be amenable to tattoos of a commemorative and superstitious nature? Could I identify port and starboard, the difference between the bow or the prow? Was I aware a ship's bathroom was called the "head"? Did I know a ship's captain—no matter how small the vessel—was allowed to marry any two people he wanted, regardless of age, or mental competency, or sex differences or similarities? Or that a captain could, if he suspected a sailor of mutinous intention, throw that sailor off into the water to drown and all without legal repercussions because out on the sea the only law is the captain's law? Did I have a loved one to leave behind and come home to, he wondered?

I answered all questions with the smallest answers possible. Mostly just nods and shrugs and "left side" and "maybe" after "maybe" after "maybe."

Near the beach in a stand of plastic palm trees, the doctor had built himself quite a ramshackle lean-to. We walked there in the twilight, as he said he could make me a comfortable place to sleep, if that's what I needed. And I did. I did need that. I needed that very much.

When we walked by citizens on strolls with their SOs and their dogs or their babies, some would throw change at our feet and smile and nod. We would scoop it up and smile and nod back. Our sun-soaked skin pegged us to them as Californians, as did our lowly and chemically becalmed states. The ease with which I tanned and refused to burn. The ease with which we ambled through the sand without stumble or hesitation. Like we were born to it. Like it was our birthright. Like our feet were evolved for sandwalking. That's a real Californian.

Then, crisis. Jenny jumped from the feather in my hair to a nickel on the ground, but the doctor got to it before I did, and a negotiation occurred. I attempted to trade other nickels for Jenny, but eventually it was the trade of a dime that brought her back to me and into my pocket.

"Fool wants a nickel for a dime," said the doctor, "far be it from me to question it. Must be some nickel."

It was. A nickel like no other. A nickel worth a dime, but to no one other than me.

The lean-to was, the doctor said, just his "This Summer" home, as he was out traveling and teaching and selling, and if I wanted, the two of us could continue traveling together for a while and return north to his real home on the southern coast of Oregon. It was, he said, a place with an extra room, and I could have that room. I had no reason to believe him that he had a real and actual home, but also no reason to doubt him, and in fact had at that point in my life decided that belief and doubt simply got in the way of living and was happy to just follow anyone who had a direction for us to go. To hell with destinations. Let's move, people.

The lean-to was fashioned from a panel of plywood, and on the side facing the world, the doctor had scrawled in white paint quite an oddball little manifesto:

EVER-REAL GOD IS LOEV & CLEAN. EVER-REAL
GOD BEGINS AND ENDS @ SOIL ON THE SKIN &
HEART IT BRIMS UP DOWN LEFT RIGHT & EV-
ER-REAL GOD PUMPS CLEAN INTO BRIMMED
HEARTS BLOOD & WASHES CLEAN WITH LOEV.
EVER-REAL BREATH ON SKIN IS LOEV THAT
FALSIFIES CONTAMINANT FOREIGN BODIE
FROM SKIN & EYES & ORGANS. DR. RIALTO
ROSE'S SAGE SOAP HERE. $5 DOLLARS.

"My advertisement," he said.

"You could use a good ad man," I said. I had, for
the shortest of times, been an ad man. Of a kind. I wrote
swatches of copy for an online retailer, and got paid by the
word. And got paid shit for the shit I sped out of my brain
and into a text document, descriptions of toothbrushes
and new compact discs and paper towels by the case. I
was a sort of an ad man and lousy at it. Six months in, my
contract was not renewed when Jenny convinced me to tell
the world a thing or two about the state of modern stitching in most commercially available Oxford shirts. (It's not
so good. It is not so good, my friends. It is bad. Stitching
nowadays is bad and that is a tragedy.)

"I need someone to help carry my pack," he said,
and pointed to the corner of the lean-to, where a military
duffel, three quarters full of little bottles with white and
green labels leaned like a drunk. Leaned like we leaned,
drunk from our afternoon. "I need a second pedaler, too,"
he said, and this time pointed to a bicycle built for two
leaning against a tree. Like another drunk. Four of us,
drunk. Together in the lean-to.

"Here I am," I said. "Let's us pedal. In the morning." And I found two comfortable spots. At the first, a little jog away, I threw up. In the second, I slept.

§

I dreamed Jenny was an infinite plane and I pedaling her length northward alone on the second seat of a bicycle built for two.

I dreamed this dream every night as Dr. Rose and I in very real life pedaled ourselves northward on his bicycle built for two from the Arizona coast to the Nevada coast to the southern coast of Oregon where the doctor claimed his house was.

We had on our ride, sold the rest of the doctor's stock of his liquid sage soap. We had started in Lake Havasu City—whose name made no sense, as it's lake was now the Pacific—and headed up to Pahrump to Carson City—whose Tahoe lake was now also not just a quaint vacation-friendly body of water, but an ocean stretching out beyond the limits of one's eyesight—to Reno to Lakeview to Klamath Falls, and finally to the doctor's digs in scenic Ashland-Newly-by-the-Sea. We rode and sold the clear plastic 8oz bottles of his goods.

In each city, the doctor found a parking lot near the beach that seemed to be a hub of activity, we parked the bike, and grabbed our soap from the bicycle's trailer, set out a blanket for the bottles, and the doctor turned over the wooden box in which he kept the stock to stand on, and from which to read from a long, handwritten script of notes concerning the soap, the nature of God, and the benefits of the former in one's journey to reach a fulfilling relationship with the latter.

Jenny was delighted as fuck. The doctor had an honest-to-goodness soap box, and he used it to stand slightly above the rest of the beachgoers, and from which to issue a speech written to convince an audience to do as the doctor wanted them to do. It was thrilling in its fealty to idiom. And what, I ask, could be more thrilling than that?

City after city, it became easier for me to identify our customers among the crowds in swimsuits and flip-flops. They were, bless their bleeding hearts, the politically left, consciously green, organic food and international music consuming, petition signing types. They were the one's who, humanity-wise, felt good about their support in general of humanity. They were the ones most likely to drop $5 or $10 when they discovered the doctor and I were Californians, not just your average itinerant, soap-slinging religious nuts. Californians. They loved us. When our state had cracked off the country and fallen into the ocean, it had—in their minds—left us in a state a grace. (And, it must be pointed out, them in a state of political dereliction. But I abhor politics, so we'll leave the seeming endless tale of politically conservative success to someone else.)

So they bought soap and they bought lunch and they bought beer and wine and liquor for us. A certain percentage of them stuck around after the sales day to ask us about our old homes, to tell us stories of the time they were in California visiting "friends," to use us to confirm or deny—though we never, ever denied, because confirmation was always more profitable—legends of the state, odd rumors about secret knowledge, or closer connections to lost storehouses of spirituality.

It was remarkable how often we spoke to them about Atlantis. How every conversation eventually turned to Atlantis. How many people seemed to believe in Atlantis. How alike was my California, I had to admit, to Atlantis. Mystery of the unknown. Some, I swear, even held out hope that our fellow Californians were down there still, breathing water instead of air, living in Utopia, waiting for an opportune moment to return and save everyone they left behind. So many whackos. All of them with money.

How was it possible that people so completely divorced from reality had so much money? What kind of a system had we developed that allowed the semi-eccentric to the batshit insane to thrive like that? Capitalism is a grade-a fucking mess, my friends.

§

Wonder of deep fucking wonders, our man the doctor really did have a little house in Ashland. Or, at least, he had the keys to a house in Ashland. And I tend to believe one and the other are near enough to be the same.

It was a squat and charmless hovel, in a squat and charming town, and it had a roof and it had indoor plumbing and it was heated—though it mostly didn't need it—by a big wood stove in the center of the place. Once it had been near the edge of the Klamath National Park, but when California disappeared into the Pacific, it became a waterfront home.

"Owners abandoned it because they did not feel up to being the owners of a beachfront home. Considered it too indulgent, I guess. Too much pressure, social-standing wise. They left an apologetic note to whomever had to take over. White people."

The doctor had been hitchhiking north when the

great quake had hit and sunk our state. He had arrived in Ashland just the night before and was sitting on a bench downtown, considering his day's activities when he felt the first tremors. And heard the tremendous snap. He felt it happen from right there near the border: the split in the earth traveling so very near the California state border, they say it was the event that made more atheists turn to God than any other event in human history. But how do they measure someone like that? How many surveys do they have to do, and how many believers would lie to pad the numbers? Did they call people on the telephone, or did they go door to door, or did they pick people at random from a mall food court? How do they know? Who did they talk to? Where was the study? Who peer-reviewed it?

And the way the state seemed to rise a little first. And the way it seemed to teeter back and forth, as if it was being slowly worked free from the country. And the way it began pulling away and the way the western border was pulled under. And the way it sped into the sea, got faster as it left. And the way so many people report hearing a collective scream, a terrified scream of the California millions as they, most at work, some at home, a few poor saps at the gym working themselves out needlessly—because in Heaven your abs are always perfect no matter how badly you eat and how sedentary your lifestyle—all screaming at once as they fell off the map and into the water. And the water filling in the space where California once was. And the way at first no one really knew what to make of it all, but when they examined their feelings, people discovered that they simply didn't care. And the way it took the sudden eyes of the world on the United States, the phone calls from international journalists asking for a reaction to the end of California, for all the Americans to pull it together, realize they were on TV, and fake some sort of distress over the loss of the third largest and most populous state in the country.

Because without the gaze of the rest of the world, most people didn't feel any real sadness at their loss. It was just a state. And some people. There were 49 more states. And we could make more Americans. People had read somewhere that most movies were filmed in Vancouver now. Washington state had a wine country. Walt Disney World was bigger and better than Disneyland. No one really would miss the Anaheim Angels or the Oakland Raiders. It was just California.

It was the way the rest of the world reacted, the way they framed it all as a tragedy that made it a tragedy for Americans. The Americans were willing to let it go.

The doctor got a house out of it. The owners had left and the Ashlandians let the doctor move in without a fuss. Poor Californian, they said to no one. He probably lost his family and all his possessions. Let's look the other way while he squats in this house. It's a small one, anyway. And waterfront. Who wants all that responsibility? Sand'll show up eventually, right, and that stuff probably gets everywhere.

I moved into the doctor's second bedroom and learned how to make the doctor's soap. It was simple enough to feel like a scam. I grated bars of cheap Ivory soap, mixed them with water and boiled them, added glycerin—just a little to keep the mixture from clumping—and a touch of white sage oil. As the doctor and I had bicycled north through Nevada, and as our pack full of bottles of soap had emptied, we'd filled the space with wild white sage from the side of the road, which at home we distilled to an oil. A drop or two for every bottle.

Jenny wanted the oil dabbed at each corner of our room, and I obliged. Then she asked that it be spread to the corners of the whole house and, surreptitiously, I obliged. Then she asked that in his sleep, the doctor be anointed with the oil—just a bit on his forehead—and, drunkenly, I obliged. The doctor, as drunk as I, slept straight through Jenny's cleansing ceremony and the speech she made me give. Our good luck.

§

IN THE TIME BEFORE NOW & THE TIME OF THE EVER-REAL GOD, WHEN THE WORLD WAS NOT MADE LIKE THE WORLD OF TODAY, EVER-REAL GOD WAS CLEAN AND LOEV & ALL REAL LOEV WAS CLEAN. CLEAN IS EVER-REAL BECAUSE EVER-REAL IS GOD AND EVER-REAL GOD COMMANDS IT. WORLD IS OPPOSITE OF CLEAN AND LOEV IS OPPOSITE OF CLEAN. OPPOSITE OF CLEAN IS ALLOWED FOR EVER-REAL GOD TO SPEAK AND SEE THROUGH LIVES OF CHILDREN AND MEN. CHILDREN AND MEN ARE OPPOSITE OF CLEAN AND CAN FIND EVER-REAL GOD THROUGH THE VOICE THAT ENCIRCLES THEIR HEARTS IN THE TIMES OF GREATEST OBLIGATION. CLEAN AND LOEV REMOVE SIGNS AND OBLIGATIONS FROM SHORT-LIVING CHILDREN AND MEN. RESEARCH INDICATES EVER-REAL GOD WORKS

IN HEARTS BUT NOT MINDS AS MINDS ARE FOREVER MADE OPPOSITE OF CLEAN. COUNT 1-2-3 FOR REMEMBERING WHEN EVER-REAL GOD IS SEEMING DISTANT.

COUNT 1-2-3 FOR WAITING WHEN APPLYING DR. RIALTO'S SAGE SOAP TO HEARTS AND BODIES FOR OPTIMAL RESULTS. MIX WITH WATER TO CLEAN THINGS OTHER THAN BODIES IN NEED. DISPOSE OF BOTTLE WITH CEREMONY. MAKE CLUTTER A CHOICE. REMOVE MINDS FROM ROOMS AND DECISIONS. EVER-REAL GOD PRETENDS YOU ARE NOT THERE SOMETIMES, TOO. EVER-REAL IS THE FORGIVENESS OF THE FORGOTTEN AND REMEMBERED HEART-BLOOD EVER-REAL GOD IN THE WIND AND IN THE SKY AND IN THE RAIN THAT FALLS ON THE EMPTY SPACE THAT ONCE AS CALIFORNIA.

$5, ALWAYS.

—On every bottle in tiny script, on a label the doctor produced by copy machine and affixed with wheat paste. And on each a little symbol, too, like an open eye with octopus arms.

"Who belongs to the eye?" I asked.

"That's God," said the doctor. "That's his present-tense manifestation. That's the one that is in the now with us."

I nodded. Jenny was more interested than I was, and shimmered across the floor in a bit of reflected light that was shining through a mobile hung with power crystals. Shimmered over to the doctor and became a thread woven in his old jeans. My nose twitched.

"The past-tense God is a thumb in the eye of the present-tense God, though. The past-tense God, with it's sense of history, enforces the rules. The present-tense God is willing to let us be who we will be, and never thinks of punishment. The past-tense God does not know a thing about who we are, or who we are going to be, or how the things we do will change as they move forward in time. The past-tense God just demands we pay."

Jenny settled in, and I found it not a bit pleasing. I could not call out to her and risk letting out into the room the fact of her existence. And, also, Jenny was not a dog or a cat and she could not be "called" as one. She had her own mind, and insisted I recognize its sophistication.

"The future-tense God doesn't even see us, or the past-tense god, or the present-tense God. The future tense God creates us, destroys us. He is the engine of life. But he doesn't know what, or care what, life is. The future-tense God isn't aware rules exist. The future-tense God is the surfer on the edge of the wave of the world."

"What were you in California?" I asked. "What did you do there?"

"The future-tense God doesn't care who I was. Why do you?"

Jenny spread out and became a whole patch of denim, and then moved up the doctor's leg.

"Just wondering. I wrote things sometimes. Freelance web content production. And in my spare time, I cashed checks from my parents. I was a shoplifter for a bit."

"Future-tense God is the God I admire the most,"

said Dr. Rose. "When you follow God, you can decide which God you most wish you could be like. I most wish to be the future-tense God."

Jenny moved up his leg and into his thigh. I sat up straighter, wondering if I improved my posture, would my Jenny notice me? I attempted contact through telepathy, but telepathy isn't real.

"I wrote horoscopes for a while. The secret was not, as you might think, to be vague. It was to be vaguely specific," I said. I stood and walked to a red plastic cooler, opened it, and reached into the ice for a can of beer, which I opened and drank in one go, reached in again, grabbed another, did the same, grabbed a third, and returned to my seat.

Jenny was moving up his thigh. She was ever so slow. "I tended bar at this place for seven weeks."

"The future-tense God," said the doctor, "is the one for me. If I could, I'd forget all the world and all the people, and I'd move forward leaving a trail of creation behind me. We're nothing but footprints," he told me. "We're nothing but wake. We're nothing but contrails. We're nothing but the after-effects of the future-tense God's move forward. He's the mechanism of the Ever-real God."

The doctor talked himself to sleep in his chair. It was big and round and looked very comfortable. It was surrounded by beer cans. He talked and his words slowed and his body slowed and he went out. And I sat across from him in a wooden chair, and I watched as Jenny moved up from his thigh to his crotch and stopped there. And, it appeared, would stay there for as long as she pleased. She did not pay attention to me again for the rest of the night. For the first time in as long as I could remember, I spent hours without her finding an excuse to become a shell in my pocket or the screw in my glasses or something in contact with me. She was on, and with, the doctor.

And he didn't even know it. I could've killed him, the anger in my hands. "I answered phones for a catalog for I don't remember how long. Eight days, maybe?"

Instead of killing this man who had taken me in, though, I puttered around the place, cleaning up messes, organizing papers, and boiling chips of soap in kettles of water and glycerin. All without Jenny.

I had not been apart from Jenny for many years. Any of the years I remember, in fact. Jenny had been my companion ever since I was a child. A little boy. A little me and Jenny. I recall clear as day Jenny as a birthday candle, coaxing me to blow her out.

Jenny on the sidelines of a soccer game, a tray holding orange slices, waiting for halftime.

Jenny as the lock on my locker, reminding me of the combination.

Jenny as a leaf in the above-ground swimming pool behind our house, waiting for me to skim her out and hold her to me.

Jenny the solution to a Rubik's cube, whispering directions.

Jenny after homecoming as Carrie Michelson's bra latch, whispering directions.

Fickle Jenny was always with me, until she wasn't. And when she wasn't? What was I supposed to do when she wasn't?

§

Framed on the wall of the Doctor's office was an old California Republic flag. Bear and bar and star. Discolored with water damage. Frayed at the edges. The interior of the frame—more a shadow box, really—had small lights to illuminate it, and the lights stayed on all the time. A waste during the day, but necessary if the Doctor was working very late and the sun was gone. The Doctor liked to work until very late. He liked to see the little lights illuminate his flag. He'd paid quite a bit for it.

His office's west wall was entirely glass so he could see the sunset. His floating desk—an unbelievable white—was attached to the north wall and spanned three quarters of the room. One would enter through a door on the east wall. The flag was to the south, and whenever I was asked to see him, Jenny made a point of being in the flag. Sometimes she was the bear. Sometimes she was the star.

"Cole," he said—because Cole was the name we chose for me when it became clear I needed a clean and empty name to offer to journalists and lawyers—"I'd like for you to tell the Soapmakers that we should stop wearing our outdoor shoes in the offices and in the factory. I've decided to provide a shoe to be worn instead. A clean shoe, Cole. One that never leaves the building. Make sure the Soapmakers know that if one of the new clean shoes is worn outside the buildings, if it is contaminated, they will lose their jobs. Can you do that for me, Cole?"

"Sure thing, Doc," I said. The Doctor hated when I called him "Doc," but I had been with him for so long, I knew he'd let it go. Any other Soapmaker called him

"Doc" and he'd can him quite thoroughly. Not me, though. And I kept at it, day after day, as my little revenge for the loss of Jenny to him. Doc this and Doc that and sure Doc and I don't know about that Doc. The board would like to meet Doc and the sales figures for this quarter are in Doc.

The clean shoe idea was a Jenny idea. Unreasonable. Confrontational. Arbitrary. A Jenny idea. She had been providing the Doctor with her ideas for a long time now. For some reason, though, in the mouth of the Doctor, a Jenny idea came out sounding feasible, implementable, good. In the hands of the Doctor, a Jenny idea was successful. It was the damnedest thing. A Jenny idea never led me anywhere but down a bad and dangerous road. A Jenny idea in me went hardcore wrong almost at the very moment of implementation.

I missed them so.

I missed those ideas. I missed Jenny striking my brain like lightning. I missed running from the cops and getting on the bad side of hotel clerks. I missed spray painting intentionally awkward sociopolitical statements on public walls or markering intentionally vile sexual come-ons on bathroom walls. I never touched a woman's breast or a man's penis without permission anymore. I never did not pay for a meal. I wasn't out breaking windows. I wasn't out peeping into windows. I wasn't even slyly masturbating in public anymore. I wasn't myself. I missed Jenny because I missed myself.

I was bored and I was boring. I had tried, for the first few years after the loss of Jenny, to continue on without her. As the Doctor and I built his little soap business, and I taught him how to smooth out some of the more eccentric edges of his presentation, I still found a moment here and there to, say, attempt a little shoplifting. But I never got caught. It was never worth it. And for some reason, I consistently stole things that were useful. Supplies for the business and such. The nerve of me.

I even got sober. I even got us sober. It took a year, and I imagined it was a thing that Jenny fought hard and harder to keep from happening, but it did. It happened. The Doctor and I in meetings. The Doctor and I having coffee after with our fellow Anonymouses.

And that's where a Jenny idea first paid off for us. One day, the Doctor shared. One day, the aura of the room, there in the hands of the voice of the doctor went anxious red to ecstatic blue to balanced and trusting green. Jenny was feeding him lines, telling him to be honest about things he wouldn't usually be honest about. Jenny was telling him to admit to things he would usually never admit. Instead of turning the crowd against him, though, the parade of embarrassing admissions and petty crimes and personal failings won the group over—as such sharing is meant to do. It worked.

After meeting, us at the table having coffee. After meeting, a woman steps to the Doctor and she is the head of our local food co-op. After the meeting, a deal is struck for the Doctor's soap on the shelves of the co-op and not just sold from a blanket on the beach in fake-ass California. And another Jenny idea goes good when the Doctor, mid-deal striking, steps forward and gives the woman a long, lingering hug. And I grab his hands and stop them as I see them begin to move down and down her back to a location on her body that would null and void that deal for sure. (As I said, I was boring.)

These hugs became a thing for the Doctor. In the hippy-dippy retail world we then entered, the hug—so very lascivious in its intention, even though I trained the attempted feel-copping out of it pretty early on—was the Doctor's point of difference, his real deal, the calling card of him as a big concept guy using the small concept of commerce to affect change in the world. That's what I told people it was. And people just bought the fuck out of that claim.

Jenny punched back by adding the gentle and wildly inappropriate whisper into the ear of the hug recipient, but damned if everyone didn't take what he said as full-hearted inspiration and eccentric compliment giving. It took a little judo now and then. "You are so beautiful. Every inch of you," was a hell of a snap to spin. "Would you like to give it a gander? It's longer than you probably think," was not as easy. Our track record? Our company history? The road we all take to enlightenment?

I got by. And the sobriety put the brakes on Jenny's most forceful presses. The Doctor in our drunken days'd have had no way to stop himself from whispering, "Drop your drawers and ride this cock for the next few hours," to our new friends in the retail world. And there'd be no coming back from that. But Jenny can only change you so much and the Doctor, when sober, was a man who had trouble with profanity.

So despite him enthralled to the giver of bad ideas, and because through dumb luck and a little bit of spin here and there from yours truly, bad ideas could be pushed into the column of surprisingly good ideas, what we found was success. Miles of success.

§

This is how it worked. The Doctor was out front, our idea and philosophy man. And I managed the Doctor. How the hell do I know how we did the rest of it? What do I know from running a business? At some point, we learned how to make soap in proper, industrial, legal ways. No more grinding existing bar soap brands into the foundation and all that. At some point, we hired people who knew how to do the day-to-day, whatever the hell the day-to-day was. Accounting, I guess. People managing, I suppose. Capitalism's scheming. My watch works but I don't know how. My business worked, but I don't know how.

But really, so much of this is lost to me in a fog of good behavior. There were meetings where people would get together around tables. There were meetings where the Doctor allowed people to tell him how to soften the edges of his image to become a more palatable figurehead for an ever expanding consumer base for his specialty product. I guess we hired and fired and promoted and retired people. We found people who knew how to do those things—research insurance packages for employees, invest capital in property and industrial machines. All that.

But I was to stand behind the Doctor. (The Doctor and Jenny.) And I was to poke at him if I saw him going too far. When Jenny wanted blood on the floor, the Doctor made to find a way to spill it, but I pulled at his sleeve and reminded him that blood on the floor was a problematic thing. I could see the Jenny in him fume. But I could see the soapmaker—the moneymaker—tighten the lid. When Jenny wanted to jump from a window, wanted to grab hold of the first close by person and jump from a window, she and the Doctor breaking their fall by breaking another's body, I would grab his hand and give it a squeeze. When Jenny wanted to fondle every single breast in a room filled with breasts, I whistled up and down, called a birdcall that refocused the Doctor, and I indicated to him that he had drool on his lip with a wipe of my own with my sleeve, the Doctor would mirror me and get back to inspiring with words.

The Jenny attacks got less and less frequent. The Jenny words and the Jenny aura, though, came easier and expanded. The Doctor to the employees. The Doctor to the investors. The Doctor to the New Californians. An army. A voting block. A lifestyle. The Doctor and his people. The Doctor's will in the world. The Doctor in profile on the cover of a magazine.

And then, a day:

"You, son, are not the pleasure you once were to be around," he said.

"I suppose this is very near to true," I said.

"You, son, are rarely of any use to me," he said.

"This is nearer true," I said.

"Your money is right. Your investments are deep here. Your life is secure. Perhaps you should not come here anymore," he said.

"You have my girl," I said. I had never spoken to anyone about her. I had never once acknowledged her existence.

"Feels like a boy to me," he said. "God's work. Moved on to bigger and better, he did. We appreciate you holding him until he found God's work to do, and God's man to do it with."

What was to say? Jenny was never coming back. I

nodded, and accepted it, and I pulled my hand from my pocket, and I offered it. And the Doctor accepted my hand in his. I shook it. I squeezed. I pulled him to me. I bit hard into his cheek. In photos, in the right light, you can still see the scar.

They disengaged me from his face and trundled me through the building. All I could see were the buzzy florescent ceiling lights, row and row and row. I could see them through the forearms wrapped around my head. There was blood on my tongue and I let it sit there. I would not swallow it. I kept it on my tongue in the parking lot, in my car, on my ride home. I kept the blood on my tongue until it dissolved.

§

The big things just roll past my eyes without me even seeing them. Sometimes, though, if I see a small spot of water on the bathroom floor, it's all I can do to keep from killing myself. Sometimes when I park a block farther away from my destination than I hope it's all I can do to keep from killing myself.

Sometimes, the tiniest, tiniest thing will bother me, and it's all I can do to keep from killing myself. Throwing away my life entirely over the tiniest, tiniest thing. That's what it's like for me.

Listen to the waves and they way they intrude the land. See this perfect, artificial beach. See my glass and my hardwood floors. An entire wall of glass looking out over the water. Dark cherry wood. See my simple, elegant furnishings. Meet my wife.

My wife. Seriously. I have a wife. And right now, I

have no earthly idea what her name is.

When I built this home, I built it as far away from the Doctor and our head office as I could possibly build it and still make it into work every day at 8am. It is one hour and—depending on traffic—twenty minutes away. Traveling the speed limit. Because, mother of fuck, I travel the speed limit. All the time, I travel the speed limit. When my kids are in the car, I travel the speed limit. Meet my kids. My kids. Seriously. They are in their rooms. Kids. Plural.

Look out across the water. A hundred or so shudders in the sea and out of it may rise a little sliver of land. And thousand more and that bit may grow or see a cousin tremble up. Ten thousand more and both might meet and head together toward the continent. A hundred thousand years from now, California might return. In this empty, uncomfortable space, California might regrow. Before the sun explodes, California might be a thing again. Stuff might get back to normal. But I'll never see it. Things will never, ever go back to normal for me.

The big things just roll past. The little things are the greatest tragedies.

When I can't remember my wife's name, I call her "Hon." When I can't remember my kids' names, I call them, "Pal," and "Little Lady."

Every night I go for a long swim. In the water, I stop and I stir my arms and legs. My arms and legs turn in serious motion as I work to keep my head as still as possible above the water. The sun falls down. I wonder how far out I could go before my body gives out and I could sink down and maybe find me some California. Maybe find an empty condo where I could live for a while. Alone.

Who walks the streets? Who sweeps the litter from

the sidewalks? Who fixes the broken windows and cleans graffiti from the walls? Who drive the ambulances? I bob in the water. Who plans the parks and cuts the ribbons? Who robs the convenience stores? Who changes the water filters? Who calls the cops to report a scream from the apartment next door? A wave approaches and I let myself float. I rise and I fall and I rise and I fall. Who is below me? Who is living in California? Who claims the dry-cleaning? Who runs for Governor? Who is holding the gun that fires the bullet that kills the man chewing on his pen behind the giant oak desk? Who?

UP NORTH

A novella

SECTION I: THE DOCTOR'S BAG

Observe it. This land was built on the body of a queen. Over the trestles built upon her gown, a train was making its way North. The destination sat in the sternum, in the cold, hard center of her. It was winter, but the tracks were littered with only feathers of snow. There was a single person in the passenger car—male, white, six feet tall, dentures (made of polished ivory in the front, wood in the back for reasons first of vanity and then cost) and a wooly overcoat lined with the moth-eaten and unwinding husk of an old, striped, brown sweater, cut up and sewed in place for reasons of layering to promote warmth. Under his seat, there was a doctor's bag. Within the bag, a doctor's implements. Sharp razors. Gauze. A bottle of alcohol for sterilization. A bottle of morphine to dull physical pain. A pair of thick, black rubber gloves. A magnifying glass. A little glowing beetle used to illuminate those crevices of the body that tend to discourage the entrance of light within them. A very small beetle used to inspect the small, small corners of the body that a man's fingers, eyes, and instruments cannot easily gain access to for inspection. A beetle with strong jaws used to break apart and ingest obstructions in the bowel or on the brain. A prayer beetle, for insertion directly in the ear of the dying to allow for the whispering of its last rites to the nearly dead, which so often have trouble hearing.

The man with the overcoat and the doctor's bag sat beneath a wooden overhang with a pocket that held his punched train ticket. North, it said. Destination: North. He worried the nail on a finger. He shook his leg in time with the sound of the train clacketing over the tracks. He swiveled his head on his neck and listened to it pop and pop and crack as it swiveled slowly around and around.

He searched the surface of his thumbnail with the tip of his tongue and the tip of his index finger. On it tiny were hills and dales and hills and dales in even, straight patterns. Mineral deficiency, it suggested. He had a mineral deficiency of some sort and it was showing in his nails. Little dry patches at the knuckles. The little hairs on the knuckles were not as stiff as they should be. He reached below the seat and pulled out his doctor's bag.

He shoveled aside bottles and instruments. Metal and wood and leather straps. Bottles and bottles—some filled with liquid, others with beetles. At the bottom, he found a tincture. For the Revitalization of the Nails and Skin of the Hand, it said. Take on the Bottom of the Tongue. Do Not Mix with Equilibrium beetles.

He reached into his ear and pulled free the Equilibrium beetle. He pulled the dropper from the bottle, and placed a drop beneath his tongue.

The beetle sat in his hand, cleaning earwax off its spindle-legs. It cared for its chin-bristles. The man looked through his bag, pushing aside more bottles and instruments, searching. When he found the jar for the beetle, he unscrewed the top and dropped the little bug into it. Then he fell asleep.

Later he turned the crank on the train's hand crank telephone and waited to hear the operator's signal. And waited to hear the operator's voice crackling through the aether. What number? What number? What number? he said to himself. What number, please? What number, please?

But the operator did not answer. No. He talked only to himself. Like some kind of crazy person. Like some kind of crazy person who talks to himself, alone on a train, heading North.

It was many days before someone else got on the train. It was a she, the man with the overcoat was almost completely, absolutely certain. He regarded the curve-in of her back and the curve-out of her front. Unmistakable. The body curves of the human female. In in back, out in front.

Yes. The man in the overcoat was terribly sure. He was a doctor. Terribly sure and an expert in the field of medicine. Terribly sure because he was an expert in the field of medicine.

The woman walked up and down the aisle of the train car three times, inspecting each seat for cushion damage, for settled stuffing, for stains that were caused by the accidental spilling of anything more untoward than coffee or perhaps brandy. The only seat to meet her standards was in the row with the man and his doctor bag, in the window seat across the aisle. The second cleanest seat in the car. Second only to the one he ad chosen.

There were, it can be pointed out, the widths of two

chairs and one aisle between the man and the woman. God has been known to frown upon such intimate distances between men and women during periods where morality is looser. Remember that. And don't be surprised if there are consequences.

Never be surprised if there are consequences, said the ticket-puncher to the woman. It's best to just go ahead and expect that there will be consequences for all kinds of behavior. Whether you carry the proper ticket or not. Whether you have asked the proper authority for permission or not. Whether you hold the properly registered license for said activity or not. Whether you have trained your body and mind to the proper preparation for the task at hand or not. In all cases, be prepared for consequences.

And how long, said the woman, have you been following this particular religious doctrine.

It's not so much a doctrine as it is God's greatest gift to us in Word-Form. And certainly, there have been over the many years of time a great many Body-Form gifts given to us by God. Certainly he has expressed a gift to us in Mouth-Words, Brain-Words, Body-Words, or Weather-Words over the years. This is the greatest, though, of the Mouth-Words. Look elsewhere, I say, for the greatest of the Brain-Words. Look to maybe the direction of Up to see the showering storm of Brain-Words.

Thank you, said the woman. I appreciate your perspective on this situation. But, really now, this was the cleanest and freshest seat available on this train, and I hardly think the man over there will in some way be able to impregnate me just because we are only a the width of two seats and an aisle's distance from one another, don't you think?

Well, said the ticket puncher

I mean, sir. Pardon, sir?

The man in the linen coat looked up from the back of his hand, which had been very much interesting him over the last couple of hours, and saw that the woman was looking at him, and beckoning his neck to turn in her direction with her delicate little eggshell wrist. Was it a fake wrist? Had she purchased this wrist? Was it a wrist implanted after a loss of the previous flesh-wrist? Because this wrist was too fair to be real. He could nearly see through it. It was enough to make the man hyperventilate a little. Ivory wrist. Flesh-wrist. Imagine.

Sir, said the woman, do you intend to impregnate me?

What?

Do you intend to impregnate me at some point during the journey?

Impregnate you with what, said the man.

This ticket puncher thinks you are sure to impregnate me with a child if I am not morally stand-upish enough. Because I am sitting very close to you by some cultural standards.

Whose, asked the man.

I don't know, said the woman.

I think I can keep from impregnating you.

Are you sure?

I am certain.

Can we swear some sort of affidavit? Would that be enough?

Who are you talking to, Miss? Me?

The ticket puncher.

The ticket puncher?

Yes, the ticket puncher.

The man looked around the train car, but was able to confirm quite quickly what he had believed to be true from a short glance. The ticket puncher was long gone.

The ticket puncher is long gone, said the man.

But I thought I was speaking to him about religion, said the woman.

I don't believe so, no.

Now the woman looked around the train car and saw that the man with the linen coat (the man with the doctor's bag) was right. The ticket puncher was and had been gone. For who knows how long.

I'm sorry, sir, she said. I often have conversations with a person's after image. I have trained my mind to remember as many details about people as possible so that, should the need arise, I can be an excellent witness for the prosecution of a crime of some sort because I am deeply committed to the assistance of victims. I remember everything about everyone I meet with remarkable detail. The side effect of which is that often those people leave and I have such an accurate memory of them, they seem to me to be still there.

Oh, said the man. That's all right. I'm sure it happens all the time.

What?

I'm sure it happens all the time.

Yes, I heard what you said. I was asking what you meant. What happens all the time?

That people remember things that accurately and then think people are still around after they have gone.

Really, she said.

Yes, I'm sure it is quite common.

The train car swayed to and fro. Outside the snow

was picking up.

I really, she said, don't think so. I've never met any-one but myself who remembers people as well as I do.

Oh, certainly, the man said.

No, but not certainly. You just said you are sure it happens all the time. As far as I know, I am the only person in the entire world who has a memory so highly trained, they sometimes think people who have left are still there. It does not happen all the time.

Well, I'm sure it doesn't, he said.

But you just said you were sure that it does happen all the time.

Oh, that, he said. Well, it was just a figure of speech.

It was?

The snow fell and fell and fell.

Yes. A figure of speech.

I don't think it was. I am acquainted with all man-ners of figures of speech, and that does not appear to be following the definition. But all right, she said. A figure of speech. For the sake of amity, let us call it a figure of speech,

The train wound long and slow through the long, slow, winding journey North.

At this rate, we could walk it, the man said one day.

Walk North? the woman said.

Yes.

No, I really don't think we could. I think this is a much faster way to travel than going by foot.

I know, said the man.

But you just said—

I was just—

Oh, she said. This is another figure of speech.

Yes, he said. I was not being serious. I was just saying.

You say often, don't you. Instead of doing other things, you just say.

I suppose that is true, the man said.

He was sitting in a new seat, the one in front of her. He had moved to the seat a day earlier. Change of venue, he said. She did not reply. Change of context, he said. She again did not reply. Change of angle, he said. Nothing. Change, he said. Snow past the window. Snow falling on the trees.

Were you a witness to a crime, he said.

What do you mean, she said.

You have trained your memory so that you can keep track of all the details of everything going on around you and you said that you did so because you wanted to be a reliable witness if you happen to be in the presence of a crime. I wondered if that meant that you had, in the past, been a witness to a crime of some consequence, and it had influenced your resolve to train yourself.

The woman furrowed her brow as if she did not understand what the man was saying.

I don't think I understand what you are saying, she said.

Possibly then you should never mind it.

Possibly, she said. I was the victim of a crime.

Oh, well, he said. That makes sense.

It does? she said

Yes. Yes, I think it does.

In what way, she said.

I think I will move back to my seat now, he said.

Isn't that your seat? I mean, you are sitting in it.

Doesn't that sort of make it your seat? Since only you and I are on the train?

Possibly, he said.

There was, as one might expect, a ghost on the train. A ghost who haunted the car inhabited by the man and the woman. A ghost who had ridden the train for decades in life and now decades after death. A ghost who was a man, but in the style of ghosts was now much more yielding to whim in its sexual characteristics.

The ghost liked to sit in the seats in the very back of the car, to listen to people talk, and to cup its ears and only half listen. It liked to fill in conversation with its own thoughts. Like, if someone said:

I believe the train is about to jump the tracks and descend to the valley below.

And the ghost cupped its ears and heard:

I believe...about to jump...descend...valley below.

The ghost would fill in the spaces and hear:

I believe this ghost is about to jump through my body and descend into my genital valley below.

The ghost was obsessed with itself and made all conversations about itself. The ghost was also obsessed with sex, and made all conversations about itself engaged in some sort of erotic behavior.

A crime happened to me, she said.

Yes? he said.

Yes. A few years ago, I was the victim of a crime.

And this is why you decided to train your memory? It had been days since they had spoken. They had willed away the time by working very, very hard to ignore one another. It had become difficult, wearying. Horrible. She tried so hard to ignore him at one point, sweat broke out on her lip. Tiny drops of sweat on her lip. All because she was struggling so hard to not talk to him, not look at him. Not think about him.

And he? Almost worse. His leg shook in rhythm with the train, but began to piston up and down violently. It caused his leg to cramp. To seize. He lost control. His leg felt close to snapping off. And then she spoke.

Yes. The crime made me train my memory.

What sort of crime was it? he asked.

A bad crime. I would prefer not to talk about it.

Were there other after-effects? Personality changes? Did you become fearful? Did you stay indoors for a long time?

I did none of those things, she said. The only after-effects are physical.

She lifted her shirt to below her right breast to show a ragged scar. The scar was a deep wrinkle, and seemed to have other scars within it.

There is still metal in here, she said. There are still pieces of metal.

Bullets? said the man.

Possibly, she said.

Bullets tend to be the only metals that one receives and keeps internally in an attack. Unless a knife point breaks off, I suppose. My professional opinion is, then, that you have a bullet inside you.

That might be true.

There was silence. Only the thunk-thunk pause thunk-thunk pause thunk-thunk of the train filled the ears.

May I check? said the man.

Check? she said.

Yes, I would like to check, he said.

And how would you do that? she said.

I would go in and check. Go in. And check.

The man pulled the doctor's bag from under his seat. He unclipped the clasp and opened the bags mouth, reached in and pulled out a scalpel. Go in, he said, poking the scalpel in her direction. Go in and check.

Ah, she said. Well, I suppose.

He started with a three-inch incision to the left of the scar. They had gone to the front of the car, to a four-seat row with a pull-down table. In an overhead compartment, they had found a tablecloth, and covered the pull-down table. They took a second tablecloth, and she covered herself from waist to toe. She pulled her shirt up to the bottom of her right breast, and lay turned on her left side.

He had pulled a Pain-free beetle and a Calming beetle from his bag, and placed the Pain-free beetle in her mouth, and the Calming beetle behind her ear. The Pain-free beetle tasted sour at first, but then she felt her mouth go numb, and then her neck went numb, and then her body went numb, and then she attempted to smile, but was so numb she was unsure if she was actually able to smile. The Calming beetle sat behind her ear humming a chord of three notes, making microtonal changes in one of them or two of them. Its legs stroked a spot behind her ear. The anxiety she felt about the scalpel disappeared before he placed it into her chest.

After the first incision, he cut two more at the top and bottom. This flap he pulled open, and he sat the scalpel on the seat next to him. Out came the Glowing beetle. He put it near the opening in her body and teases it with his fingertip. Get in, he said. Go on, get in. The beetle turned to him, but he used his finger to spin it back around and he repeated: Get in. Get in there. Cajoled, the beetle entered the cavernous incision.

He followed the beetle in with a pair of forceps. The beetle walked through the muck of the interior of her body, through the meat and bubbles of fat, and the slick trails of heavy blood. Through the winding trail left by whatever it was that had at one time entered her body. The beetle followed the cave in the flesh, which was old enough that the muscle was mostly grown back in. Like vines cut away with a machete, a trail created through a jungle, and left to its own, things had grown back to cover the way over. But a little bit remained. A little bit of the trail was still there. The beetle was adept at re-blazing a trail through the body. The forceps followed behind.

The beetle came to a point where the trail split, and felt around with its chin. It felt and rubbed and determined the larger of the two trails and followed it deeper into the body. The forceps followed.

An hour into its journey through the trails in the woman's body, the beetle stopped for a rest. The forceps stopped, too. The beetle ran a leg through a puddle of blood, and licked the fluid from it. It did so two more times, filling its mouth with the blood, coating its throat.

A man approached the beetle. Can I help you find something, he said?

No, she said. I'm taking a walk down this trail. I am looking for the end of it, but I don't think I need anyone to point the way.

Well, he said. If you insist. I will leave you to it.

Actually, she said, if you would stay for a moment.

The man had a backpack and a walking stick. The end of the stick was covered in gore. He set the stick down and sat next to her. Are you lonely? he said.

A little, she said.

He clicked his tongue at the beetle, and placed his hand on her thorax. There, there, he said. All will be well.

How long have you been hiking? she said.

Not long, he said. A year. Two, maybe. Just walking around, taking everything in.

Is this place safe? she said.

Oh, not in the least. It is very, very dangerous. I have managed to survive because I am smarter and stronger than most every creature in here. But I have only just barely survived. You would do well to spend as little time as possible here.

He continued to rub her thorax gently. Back and forth, back and forth. It felt very nice. She doubted his warnings. She dug her legs into the wet, sticky floor beneath her, and she considered taking a little nap. But then the forceps poked her hindquarters.

I think your pet would like to go, he said.

That's not my pet, she said.

What is it, then? he said.

I cannot be entirely certain, she said, but I believe that that is God.

Pity his creations, then, he said.

Yes. Please do. I know I do, she said.

She walked on down the path. When she came to a second trail split, she chose incorrectly—though her senses insisted she should choose the path she chose—and found a dead end. When she turned, she saw a lump. When she studied the lump, she saw that it was moving. When she backed away, she saw the lump advance on her. When she tried to get by it, she found herself blocked. So she stopped moving. And the lump approached.

May I help you, she said.

The lump replied, No, not at all.

May I get by you, she said.

The lump replied, No, not at all.

Then we seem to be stuck.

The lump replied, Yes, we are stuck, and stuck for good.

But I have to find something, she said.

The lump said, That is not my problem.

I might pray, she said.

The lump said, You do what you think is best.

So she prayed and she waited. And she prayed more, and she waited. Where had the forceps gone? They were nowhere, it seemed. They had been following her, but now they were gone.

What is your name? she said.

The lump said, I really don't think I have one. But you could check, couldn't you?

How do I check? she said.

The lump turned over and she saw that it was flat beneath. There, it said. It might say under there.

She approached the lump and peeled back a fold in its body. Nothing under here, she said.

The lump said, Could you dig in deeper? It might be hidden. Names are often hidden.

If you insist, she said. She dug a little deeper into the lump and she felt around and felt around. The inside of the lump felt like the outside of the lump. It felt wet and warm. It felt sticky. It felt smooth. She dug in deeper. Her legs felt warmer as she dug to its center. And then she felt something solid and rough.

I think I have something, she said. Can I pull it out?

The lump said, Yes, please. Remove it.

She pulled the something free and found that it was a rectangular metal plate. On the plate, it said: Donald.

This says Donald, she said.

The lump said, Do you suppose that's my name?

Yes, she said. I suppose that is your name.

The lump said, How entirely disappointing. I've never liked the name Donald. I suppose there is nothing to do about it, though. You are who you are.

The forceps appeared from up the path and they jabbed into Donald. The lump made a noise like steel wool on a pan, a terrible screech, and the was snipped into two lumps. And then four. Then six. Then the little pieces melted.

God takes his time, she said.

The trail widened and narrowed. It grew taller and shorter. It went straight for maddeningly long length, or curved so many ways, it felt to her that the tunnel had doubled back impossibly into itself, or spiraled and spiraled and spiraled. Long climbs up and long slides down.

And then she came to the end. There it was: a jagged piece of metal. Well, she said to the forceps, it looks like we've made it. She guided the forceps to the shrapnel. They clinked against it, turned clockwise and then counter-clockwise feeling for an edge. And when they found one, they opened wide, and slowly bit down.

The end of the tunnel filled with lumps. A dozen at least. She turned to the forceps, but they were busy pulling the shrapnel free. When she turned back, the first of the lumps rolled to her, divided in the front, and covered her leg. And then another did another leg. And another. A lump hopped up onto her hindquarters and its weight pulled her down. another anchored that one. Another jumped to the middle of her shell and melted in. Another and another followed and her legs buckled. Another hopped onto her head and covered her eyes. Through a blur of melting flesh, she saw the forceps pull free the shrapnel and pull out of the tunnel. Her glow was dimming. She watched the ends of the forceps and the shrapnel disappear into the dark. She forgot to say anything. She completely forgot. Everything went black.

He was standing over her with a pair of forceps. In the jaws of the forceps, a little shard of metal.

Well, I got it, he said.

Stay still while I sew up the flap, he said.

The Calming beetle's song will get a little faster soon and it will pull you back to complete consciousness, he said.

This shouldn't leave a scar, he said.

The Pain-free beetle has probably dissolved by now, he said. You may notice a strange odor to your urine for the next week or so. Like sage. That is normal. You are not anymore unhealthy than you were when your urine didn't smell like sage. Just remember that.

You were praying to the forceps, by the way, he said.

Am I awake? she said.

Yes, indeed, he said. Sewn up, free of this little thing, and the Defense beetle should stave off infection and keep most of the scar tissue away, too. You should heal up good as new.

Thank you, she said.

It was my pleasure, he said.

It was nearly sunup. There were suggestions of dawn at the horizon. She sat up and looked at her legs and arms. The train rolled on and on, heading North.

Through the magnifying glass, he studied the metal object he had removed from her body. It's a bullet, he said.

It was a bullet? she said.

Yes. This is unmistakably a bullet.

What sort? she said.

What do you mean? he said.

What sort?

What caliber? she said. I'm afraid, he said, that my bullet identification skills do not stray much past the 'this is a bullet' line. I am unsure what caliber. Medium?

Medium, she said, makes sense. It felt medium entering me.

He turned it over and over, carefully searching the surface. He held it in a pair of forceps, and had set the magnifying glass on his seat's tray table in a stand with elbowed armatures. He held a thin pointed pick in his other hand, and tapped at the surface of the bullet.

I think there is a crack in the surface. A split of some sort, he said.

Where? she said.

Here, he said, pointing to a line in the surface. Do you see?

Yes, she said. I think I see that.

Hold the forceps, he said.

She did so. She held the forceps and he reached into the bag and pulled out another pick like the one he was already using to explore the bullet's surface. Hold it steady, he said.

He placed the points of each pick into the crack in the surface, and tried to separate the bullet. It would not give at first. It would not give when he tried a second time. But a third time managed to open the crack a little. More tugging separated the surface more. And more. Inside the mangled bullet there was something. He pulled and pulled, and broke the bullet in half.

He reached into his bag and pulled out tweezers. The bullet was hollow, and inside one half was something. Paper, it seemed to be. A slip of paper. Tiny. She held the half of the bullet with the slip of paper up to the magnifying glass, and he pulled the paper free with the tweezers.

He lowered the magnifying glass, and placed the paper on the tray. He used the tweezers to flatten the paper.

Try not to breathe heavily on the tray, he said.

I will try, she said.

We don't want the paper being carried away.

Yes, I know, she said.

It looks like it has something on it.

Yes, she said.

Something written.

I think so, she said.

Words.

A word, she said.

Yes, he said.

Bang, it said. The slip of paper had the word Bang on it.

Try the other side, she said. He turned the slip over with the tweezers. There was something there. Another word.

Remember? he said. It says Remember?

Yes, she said. I do.

The man cranked the phone. What number please? What number? What number please? Please? Please? But still there was no answer from the operator. This trip lasts forever, he said.

No, she said. I have taken it before. If it lasted forever, I would still be on the first trip, not this second one. Do you see?

Yes, he said. I do see. Thank you for pointing that out.

You are very welcome, she said. She turned to look out the window.

I did not mean that literally, he said.

I'm sorry? she said.

I did not mean that the trip was taking forever literally. I was simply pointing out that we have been traveling for a long time and don't seem to be getting any closer to the city.

Oh, she said.

Oh, he said.

I guess it didn't occur to me that you were not speaking literally, she said.

Really? he said. It didn't occur to you?

No, she said. I was taking you at your word.

Well, you will forgive me, madam, but that is the stupidest thing I have ever heard. How the hell could I be speaking literally if I was speaking of forever in that manner! It would be impossible for a journey to last forever. Impossible. If it was a journey that lasted forever, it would not be a journey because a journey pre-supposes a destination. A trip that takes forever cannot have a destination. And therefore cannot be a journey. Do you see?

We're here, she said,

I'm sorry? he said.

We have pulled into the station. Our journey has reached its destination. You can get off the train now.

At this moment, this very important moment, the ghost stuck its tongue in the man's ear, and its fingers between the folds of the woman's genitalia. (A ghost can, when it wants, take up as much or as little room as it wishes.) This caused both man and woman to let out a sigh, a relieved sigh. An erotic sigh. An unexpected sigh.

The ghost spun its tongue in the man's ear, and this was a distraction. He forgot his anger at the woman's obtuseness and pulled his doctor's bag from beneath his seat, buttoned up his coat, and stepped off of the train.

The woman, still being deeply fingered by the ghost, stood, too, and followed the man. In her pocket, she had a small glass vial. In the vial, the slip of paper with the words. Bang. Remember.

SECTION II: MOURNING

At the station, she caught a cab. When provided with the address of their destination, the driver turned to her.

One of those, he said.

I'm sorry? she said.

You, he said. You're one of those people.

I'm not sure what you mean, she said.

The club. You're going to one of those clubs, he said. Let me just say that I will take you there, but I would prefer it if you would not speak to me during the ride, okay? I like to consider myself, he said, an open-minded person. And I think that if there are certain things that help people get through their day to day lives, then I try not to judge them. But I think the clubs are, frankly, kind of sick. That's it. I'm done speaking to you. This is the last word I will say. This.

Perhaps, she said, since you have asked me to extend you the courtesy of not speaking to you, you will extend me the same courtesy.

I have said my piece, he said. I think your choice is objectionable, and I feel like I need to say that. This.

The driver turned and pulled the car away from the station and took her to her destination. They remained silent.

They arrived at a building which was just like every other building. It had walls, windows, a door, some steps. It had people. It had signs. It had a rear entrance. She entered through the rear entrance. She saw a counter. She walked to the counter.

I'd like a booth, she said.

The clerk asked for a small amount of money which she handed over without attempting to haggle.

Did you want a boy or a girl, the clerk said.

Girl, she said.

Of course, said the clerk. Booth 17 should be open. Blond is okay?

Blond is fine, she said.

It's down the hall on the left, said the clerk.

She walked down a long, dark hall, passing booths. Quiet sobbing could be heard behind most of the doors, but behind one or two, full-throated wails erupted and she flinched when she heard them. The hallway had a grade to it, a decline. She got farther back into the building, and was heading deeper into the ground. Booth 17 was the last booth before a left turn that continued on, deeper and darker, and further into the ground.

Booth 17 had a fading color photograph of a little blond girl under the room number. It had a tear in the corner. A water stain in the sky. A little girl standing, impassive face, arms to the side. A white dress with blue flowers. Short hair over small, prominent ears. She had a cleft chin and bright blues eyes. A tiny nose. A round face. Her mouth was slightly open, and there was the white of two front teeth. She was standing on a porch on the top step next to a pot of washed-out red begonias. The stairs were blue. She held a miniature pinwheel. She was not posing, just lost in thought. Just having her picture taken. Just that.

The woman touched the photograph with her thumb, smoothed it down. One of its edges had worked free of the white putty that had affixed it to the door. Smoothing it out re-affixed it. She opened the door.

The booth was dark. There was a single chair and

a screen and a box next to the chair with a coin slot. The woman sat down in the chair and put her purse on her lap. She fished out some coins and she fished out some tissues. She put the tissues in her lap. She counted out the coins and put them on the arm of the chair. She dropped the first coin into the coin slot, and a movie flickered to life.

A black title card with writing appeared. Molly, age 2 years, it said. And then Molly, the little girl from the photograph walked into a living room. She looked tired, like she had just woken up from a nap. Behind her was a man, a father likely, but his head was cut out at first, and when he leaned down to encourage the little girl to enter the room, his face was blurred. The film was silent. He motioned for her to go ahead.

She was wearing the dress from the photo and a large brown cardigan. Her face was flat, still a little puffy from her nap. She looked at the camera and around the room. The camera panned around and there were people there. All had blurred faces. Some looked to be clapping. Some were gesturing for the little girl to enter. They were seated in chairs in a semi circle. The camera panned to a table covered in wrapped boxes. Bows. Another table with cupcakes and a bowl full of chips. A punch bowl. The camera panned back to the little girl and her face began to tighten a little. She smiled a little. Her eyes went bright a little. She walked into the room, and as she passed, people touched her shoulder. Tousled her hair. She walked into the arms of a woman who was kneeling next to a chair. They hugged. The little girl turned and walked to the camera, her face getting very close. She smiled at the camera.

The woman pulled a tissue from her lap and dabbed at her eyes. She was beginning to tear. Sweet girl, she said aloud. Sweet little girl.

The film continued. A birthday party. The little girl opened presents her face happy sometimes, curious the next, serious and determined the next. She held up gifts and people applauded. She handing books to the blur-faced woman next to her, and the woman held the books opened and gestured at images and text within. She held a stuffed butterfly aloft, stood with it, walked it to a party-go-er, held it out proudly, smiled. People touched her shoulders. People rubbed her back.

The woman was crying. Poor, sweet girl, she said. I'm so sorry. I'm so very sorry.

The little girl ate cake happily. She sat in people's laps. She smiled and twirled. She held hands with people. She reached out for everyone and everyone reached back. I'm so sorry, the woman said. I'm so sorry, sweetie.

It's all a lie, she thought. It can be so hard. It can be so hard to live. You didn't ask to live. You were forced into it. And then you were made to believe, she thought, that it was going to be like this. But it's not going to be like this. I'm so sorry we lied to you.

The woman wept. Sometimes the film flickered out and she added another coin. It was on a loop. She watched it for an hour, and she cried.

When she was finished, she walked to the bathroom and wetted a paper towel. She washed her face with it and closely examined her eyes. They were red at the rims and filled with tears. She washed off what remained of her makeup and reapplied it. She brushed out her hair and put it up in a ponytail. She straightened and smoothed her clothing. She brushed the lint from the back of her skirt.

And satisfied she had set herself straight, she returned to the counter.

All finished? said the clerk.

Yes, I believe that will do, she said.

I hope that helps, said the clerk.

I think so, she said. Can you call me a cab?

Sure, said the clerk.

The driver of the one I took here from the station was very rude to me, she said. Do you think you can find someone a little more sympathetic to this?

Of course, said the clerk. We know of a few who are more friendly to our kind. Just have a seat over by the door and someone will be along to pick you up in a few minutes.

How was your visit? the driver said.

Therapeutic, she said. Quite therapeutic.

Can I ask you a sort of personal question about it? he said.

Only if you don't expect me to answer, she said.

It's just something I always wonder about people, he said. I spend a lot of time driving people to and from that place. And I like to ask the people a question. I tell them they don't have to answer. You don't have to answer. He drove with his eyes in the rearview mirror, paying attention to her instead of the road. But the road was empty. And straight. It was a long, straight, deserted road from the club's district to her next destination.

Go ahead, she said.

It's just this thing that I wonder. I wonder about who people pick. Like, here. I'll start. For some reason, I need to go to see girls, three or four years old. And redheads whenever possible. Those are the ones I need to see to really let everything out. And so I ask other people who they pick. Do the men usually pick men? Do the women just pick women? Do you ask for ones who are, racially speaking, the same? Or do you want someone different? You know? Do you pick you? Or someone else who is nothing at all like you? That's what I wonder. Like I said, though. You don't have to answer.

He looked in the rearview, and she looked up, and they looked in each other's eyes. He raised his eyebrows, and cocked his head. She looked at him. And then she looked away. Blonds. Girls. Two years or so old, she said.

So you pick you?

Yeah, she said. I guess I do. I pick me.

One year, she got a kite. It was a box kite with a rainbow pattern. It had long tails. The sides had faces. Angry, angry faces. Eight faces. They seemed to object to one another, and when she would take the kite out to the park to fly it, the faces would begin to bicker with one another.

You shut up.

No, you shut up.

No, you shut up.

No, you shut up.

No, you shut up.

No, you shut up.

No, you shut up.

No, you shut up.

Around and around it went. She tuned the kite out as well as she could, but the endless angry incantations circled and circled and circled in her brain. And it got shriller and shriller and shriller. Always the faces fought with one another. Constantly they bickered like brothers. (Or like she was led to believe brothers bickered. She was an only child and preferred the company of other only children. On rare occasions, she would befriend someone with a single sibling—never more than one. But those relationships were doomed. She felt teamed up on.)

I would like to face front.

No, I would like to face front.

You always face front. I think it is my turn to face front.

I'm sick of facing front upside down and would like the kite turned over.

The kite can't be turned over because the tail is on your end. You and the other four are the bottom.

How dare you use the word 'bottom' to describe where the four of us are. It's that kind of subtle hierarchical language use that proves what a classicist you are.

This is precisely the kind of conversation that gets us nowhere, gentlemen. And it's classist. Not classicist. A classist discriminates based on social class. A classicist studies the ancients.

Always trying to play the peace-maker. And always showing off. Always trying to suggest that you are somehow superior to the rest of us intellectually and spiritually because you manage to see through our 'petty' squabbles. This is why we all hate you the most.

And where do you get off calling us 'gentlemen?' We have no primary or secondary sexual characteristics and could well decide we want to self-identify as either gender. I'm sick of you oppressing me.

I'm, frankly, sick of all of you and all your worthless talk. Why can't we have a day, an hour, even a moment of silence?

Yes, right. So you can 'meditate' on some sort of

important conceptual framework for your manifesto.

I'm sick of that manifesto. You can't even put it down on paper. You can only deliver it and hand it down through the oral tradition, and since we are the only kite this little girl owns, there's no chance you'll be able to propagate it. No one will hear it. None of us care to memorize it.

At least I am trying to do something with my time. At least I have goals. At least I feel like my life has meaning!

Enough, she screamed. Enough, enough, enough. And they would quiet down for a short time. But soon they would be back at it.

The kite's eight faces wouldn't even stop to enjoy flight! It was remarkable. A tragedy. They floated above the park on beautiful Spring and Summer days, over the green fields and the trees, and they floated near the gentle cloud cover, but saw none of it. Fought and bickered and huffed. It was too much to bear. Eventually, she flew the kite in a strong Autumn windstorm, and when a gust pulled it from her hand and out into the trees where it was torn to shreds by the bare branches, she did not once feel regret.

The driver scurried the little car through the streets, tossing and turning the wheel to find the woman's destination.

This is a nice place you're staying while you're here, he said. A nice, nice place.

Noting that he was looking in the rearview mirror, she satisfied his comment with a nod. The city, North, slipped across the window. The streets were edged with slush. The trees had bowler hats of white snow, as did the mailboxes and the fire hydrants. And sometimes also the people. There were people on benches who hadn't moved in days, and they had halos of snow. They had stovepipe hats of snow. A man on a bench had a tower of snow on his head that reached as tall as he was. He was sitting with his head resting on his fists.

Some people wait out the weather? she said.

Yes, it seems the best thing to do when it gets like this, he said. We get, some of us, a little phlegmatic when the weather turns. Both in mood and in anatomy, too. Some find themselves so filled with thick, sluggish fluid in their sinuses, they can barely lift their heads from their pillows.

This conversation has started exploring cavities I'd rather not explore, she said. Do you mind if we spend the rest of the ride not talking?

Oh, said the driver. Yes, I think I can do that. I apologize.

Not at all, she said. The body is of interest to many, many people. I feel a little too close to it right now, though. I recently had invasive surgery.

The rest of the ride was conducted in complete silence. The driver was kind enough, even, to slow his breathing to a near complete stop. He inhaled and exhaled with such minimal physical strain, it quieted even the scraping together of the fibers of his clothing when his chest barely rose and even more barely fell.

Destination reached, she removed herself from the cab after paying the driver, and took the stairs to the building slowly. One at a time. Step after step. She pressed a button to ring a bell. She waited for someone to let her in.

To the door came a long-chinned man in a charcoal gray suit. He extended a hand as he held the door open.

You are Dinah? he said.

I am Dinah, she said.

The lawyer will see you in his office.

She was escorted through smoke and burgundy-colored hallways, placed in a smoke and burgundy-colored elevator, greeted by a short-chinned, wide-eyed man two floors up, and led through another smoke and burgundy-colored hallway to a deep brown door. A simple door. A flat, perfectly smooth door. You may knock and you may wait, Dinah, said the short-chinned man.

I will do that, she said. And so she did. She knocked and she waited. And she waited.

The door swung open soundlessly. A man with a high forehead and no eyebrows stood before her. He was balding up the center of his head. The long forehead, the lack of eyebrows, the open expanse of scalp, the paleness of his skin, a thin layer of moisture, and the dimness of the lighting made him look, from the eyes up, like a recently de-fleshed skull. As did the receding gums that appeared to barely hold in his teeth. Below the mouth, though, a heavy chin beard, long and braided, trailed to his belly and swung and looked to her like a sign of life.

Dinah, he said.

Mr. Morgan, she said.

A sad day, he said.

The sad day was a week ago, she said. Today is simply a day to tie up loose ends.

So it is, he said. Let's get the key.

He walked to his desk, his beard swinging out when he turned a quick 180, and sat in a large leather chair. The chair squonked and chirled like grated teeth when his weight rested upon it. He opened a drawer and pulled out a manilla envelope. You are to read the enclosed letter here, and then I am to throw it in the fire, he said. He pulled free the letter, and then turned the envelope over, shook it, and it produced a key. And this will let you into your uncle's house.

She sat in a chair in the corner of the room, another buttony leather affair, and she read the letter from her uncle.

Dearest Sadie, it began

Many years ago I hid something for you. Something you wanted no one to find. No one found it, Sadie. No one ever found it. Just like I promised.

Now I would like you to hide something for me. Hide my home. Hide it entirely and forever. Hide it because there is too much there that I don't want anyone else to find. Hide it. You know how.

You may balk at this request. I realize that. So I have added some incentive. It is there, Sadie. In the house, and in a place where you will never be able to find it. They are coming to the house and they will be there soon. You can look and search and you will not, will not find it, so what you will have to do to keep it hidden for good and forever is that you will have no choice but to hide the house.

Hide the house, Sadie. It will be bad for my reputation if you don't, and I would think that that would be something to you. But maybe it's not. Maybe my reputation is not something to you. Maybe it's nothing to you. So, instead of it simply being bad for my reputation, instead it is—the house—dangerous to you.

Hide the house, Sadie. Hide the house.

Your loving uncle.

Which way to the street, she said.

You don't remember, said the man.

Not anymore, no, she said. I don't remember how I got in here. I don't remember how to leave. I need to leave. I need to leave right now. Please tell me how to leave.

You seem, said the man, to be agitated.

I am agitated, she said, and I need to leave this building. Please tell me how to do that as quickly as possible.

Well, said the man, I would think that the quickest possible way to leave the building would be to jump from the window. But we are up very high. It's quite likely that jumping from the window would kill you. You're not interested in dying as a consequence of gaining egress from the building, are you?

No, she said. I just need to leave.

Well, not out the window, then, he said. Though it is certain to be the quickest way. By quite a bit, actually. The other ways of getting out of this building are not as fast. This hallway, for example.

The man opened a small concealed door in the panel behind the desk. It opened on a small hallway. There were small light fixtures and small paintings on the wall.

Follow this to the end, he said. You will find an exit that way. Never turn right, though. Take every left turn to find the way out. The right turns will be mistakes. Don't make them.

She agreed. She hunched over and crawled into the small hallway and made her way down it. She was, as the man said, careful to only take left turns.

The hallway went on and on, and the left turns continued and continued.

And continued.

SECTION III: HER FOOT

In her big toe, a tiny beetle was rummaging. The little beetle had lost its way. It was tasked with caring for, with nurturing, with cultivating within her chest cavity, a garden. In the garden grew herbs that helped the beetle help the woman regulate her moods. In the garden grew herbs that helped the beetle help the woman regulate her blood pressure and her cholesterol. In the garden grew herbs that helped the beetle help the woman get rid of a headache when she had a headache. In the garden grew herbs that helped the beetle help the woman abort unwanted—and they were all unwanted—pregnancies the very morning after conception had occurred.

The beetle, the little Farmer beetle, was lost in her foot. Within his jaws, he grasped a cutting from one of the plants. It was supposed to be delivered to her optic nerve. It, when applied to her optic nerve, was meant to increase the sensitivity to light of the signal running from the nerve to the brain. It was meant to help her see better in the dark. She was in the small hallway and it was dark. The beetle was trying to assist.

But the beetle, the little Farmer beetle, was lost in the woman's foot, and it did not know how it had gotten there.

Let me tell you how it got there. It lost its sense of direction and took a right when it was supposed to take a left.

The beetle, the little farmer beetle, was growing old. It had been nurturing the plants in the woman's chest cavity for many years. A beetle does not live so long. A little Farmer beetle lives longer than most, but still, not so long. The little Farmer beetle was having trouble remembering things. It was having trouble placing itself inside the woman's body. It had trouble reading the words on the signposts that had been set up in the woman's body so it knew which way to go when the woman needed the beetle's assistance.

And lately, the beetle had been delivering the wrong herbs to the wrong places in the body. Like, say, one time, the beetle was informed that it needed to bring a blood-clotting herb to a cut above the woman's left breast. This was an easy task. The garden was very close to the left breast. The blood-clotting herb was one of the most easily recognized herbs, smelling as it did of oranges and slightly fetid rainwater. Looking as it did: a chain of purple flowers. It was, in the garden, well marked. Familiar. Known well to the little Farmer beetle.

But his mind was going. Age was taking his mind away. Age was pulling away sections of his mind, places he visited often. And he became confused when he was told to bring the blood-clotting herb to the cut above her left breast. And instead, he gathered a cutting from the garden, and took a bad turn, and delivered instead a herb that stimulated sad memories to the woman's heart.

And there she was, dabbing at the blood flowing from the cut above her left breast, the cut placed there by a kitchen knife that she had fumbled when pulling it from its block. And there she was with a sad memory stirring not in her mind—where a sad memory goes—but in her heart. Her heart beat stronger and slower for a moment. And another moment. She dropped the kitchen towel she was using to stanch the blood from above her left breast. She dropped it and felt at her heart.

The organ slowed, confronting its sad memory. It beat off rhythm, confused; so confused by this strange sensation spreading through it. The heart felt like it wanted to cry, but a heart can't cry. A heart doesn't have the necessary tools, the plumbing needed, to cry. Instead the heart beat a sad rhythm. It beat in groups of three instead of groups of two. Lub dub dub, rest. Lub dub dub, rest. It expanded and then did two half contractions, and then it sat for a long moment, considering its options. Would it beat again? The heart was like a coughing, shuddering face. It moved like a head held in someone's hands. The valves sighed and whimpered.

It was so pathetic, the lungs became infuriated. They chastised the heart for it's lack of emotional resolve. But they were lungs, and had no voice with which to chastise. (The vocal cords were indifferent to it all, busy instead considering how to convince the woman to hum so they could have something to do.) The lungs showed their displeasure by squeezing in on the heart. They gave each other a signal, and squeezed in close, crowding the shuddering heart.

But what they had intended to be read by the heart as admonition, the heart read instead as an attempt to comfort it. And this embrace by the lungs gave the heart a moment's rest from its sad memory, long enough that it was able to banish the sad memory and begin pumping blood normally. The blood, up to that point dazed by the change in the familiar pattern of its swimming from place to place in the body, settled happily back to its work.

All because the beetle, the little farmer beetle, was getting old. Old and confused.

And now it was stuck in her foot with an herb meant for her optic nerve. No optic nerve in sight. Almost as far away from it as possible. And no one to ask for directions. Instead, it went to sleep, and dropped the herb from its mouth.

Her foot felt numb. She had made her way through the tunnel, and felt her foot go numb, and felt herself distracted by the numbness. She pulled her foot up to her chest and rolled onto her back. She pulled her shoe from her foot and rolled it away down the tunnel. She pulled her sock from her foot and rolled it into a ball she set next to her. She pulled her foot to her mouth and rolled her tongue around the big toe.

The toe was coated with saliva. She waited as it dried. It dried slowly, ever so slowly, but she waited. An hour went by.

When her toe had dried, she scratched at the skin with her thumbnail. Her thumbnail was long and well-manicured. Rounded perfectly at the tip. And also it was quite sharp. She had worked the tip to a sharp edge. She scratched the dried skin, covered as it was with the leavings of her dried saliva, an chemical-rich compound that made the skin thinner and weaker, that worked to make the connections between the skin cells weak. And the layers of skin flaked off. She scratched every bit of skin free from her toe, leaving a wet red digit, alive with pain.

This woke her foot up. The little tentacles of pain reached out from the big toe and into every other numb little toe. They reached across the numb foot and into the numb ankle. Her foot woke to the pain.

She searched with her hand until she found the sock, and pulled it back on her foot. She crawled forward, a hand searching in front of her, until she found her shoe. She placed the shoe back on her foot and retied the laces.

The pain in her foot split her concentration between tunnel and foot. But it also gave more of her brain over to both. In this way, the pain in her foot helped her find her way through the tunnel and back out into the street in front of the lawyer's office. Once outside, she watched the street to see if she could find another taxi.

It was still snowy. She stood beside the road under a bus stop awning with a hand raised to hail a taxi, but the streets were so free of vehicles of any kind, and especially of taxis, that she spent a long, long time in that position. Eventually, her raised hand was covered in snow. (There were, I should've pointed out a sentence or two ago, no longer busses in the city. The busses had been sold off at the beginning of winter because it was determined that they were much more trouble than they were worth, what with their larger than normal tires and their larger than normal windshield wipers. The little bus stop awnings, though, were still around because they were a popular place to stand waiting for taxis or rides from friends.)

She considered the tiny hill of snow that had formed on her hand. Of what use was it? Could she find one? Could she form it into a snowball? Was it wet enough for proper packing? Could she throw it across the street at the windows of the house there and get the attention of the people living there? Would those people use their telephone to call her a cab if she managed to get one of them to come out and ask her why she had thrown a snowball at their window?

And where was she going? She pulled a black notebook from her coat pocket and checked the address of her uncle's house.

It was, it turned out, the house across from the lawyer's office. She was already there. Fate had offered her a kindness. She wondered how to repay it. Possibly, later, she would sacrifice something to it. A tufted black Winter Sparrow, maybe. Fate enjoyed the sacrifice of sparrows. There were so many of them. They were prolific breeders. They were a bit of an affront to fate in that way. Fate liked it when they died.

Limping, she crossed the street to her uncle's house. The key fit the lock, but she considered the possibility that this was mere coincidence.

(Oddly, it was.)

SECTION IV: HER UNCLE'S HOUSE

It is very important here for me to make clear the distinction our culture makes between a "house" and a "home." Or at least to remind you of it. Very important.

A "house" is a place where people live out their ordinary lives. A "home" is a place where one goes when one has something interesting they want to do. One must, of course, have access to both. One has one's house, and one keeps all one's stuff—one's clothes and one's cookware—there. One leaves one's house, say, once a week, though, and goes to one's home, where one does something of note. One might, say, carry on an affair in one's home if it is true that back at one's house, one has a spouse of some gender or another. One might, say, go to one's home when one decides that it is high time to commit some sort of suicide, because suicide is about the most alive thing one can do, and doing so in one's house is an affront to real, honest living. One might, say, take a bottle of champagne with one to one's home, drink the entire thing, call a delivery boy, have two more bottles of champagne delivered, drink half of the next bottle, turn on the radio, find a song one likes, and dance without embarrassment—and, it is important to point out, without an audience—to said song, maybe also belting out the lyrics to the song (if the song is one of those songs that has singing in it) while holding the half-empty bottle of champagne in one's hand, and swaying it furiously without ever spilling a drop. One might, say, when one's water has broken and one's contractions are spaced close together, go to one's home to deliver one's baby in one's clawfoot tub under the supervision of a professional midwife—or, if one is really trying to live, one might do so under no professional medical supervision at all, and one might cut one's umbilical cord from one's baby with one's incisors!

This is the difference between a "house" and a "home." I remind you of the difference between a "house" and a "home" because her uncle's house was his house and his home both. Her uncle's house was unique in that way. History had never seen anything like it before, and never would again. Her uncle's house was his house and his home and it had to be destroyed because of it. Because it was a blasphemy with a roof, and a kitchen with a gas stove, and two and a half bathrooms, and a breakfast nook, and three bedrooms, and an attic.

The door opened quietly. The entryway was dark. She removed her shoes and left them on a small rack beside the door. She removed her coat and left it on a hook over the rack. She removed her scarf and added it to the coat hook. She did not remove her calfskin gloves. Instead, she pulled them on tighter.

The house of her uncle had not changed, she thought, but little light sifted in through the cracks in the curtains, and she had not turned on any lights, so she may have been mistaken. It just, in the dark, seemed the same. But her memories of the place were dim. Perhaps the dimness of the light fooled her by suggesting—metaphorically—its connection to the dimness of her memory. This happened to her often. She had a strange neurological condition that made connections like that—that connected states of being with unrelated states of emotion that shared common signifiers. She believed that a wool sweater she had purchased at a second hand store was in some way connected to a fuzzily remembered event from her girlhood—something about a St. Bernard and a wooden fence and a plastic bucket. She believed that a loose bolt barely holding a mailbox to a post was an indication that the person who received mail at that location was promiscuous. It could all be very confusing for her, but she managed to integrate these lapses into her world-view after years of thought experiment and private behavioral training. She willed sense out of her perceptions of the world.

Another coat was hung on the coat rack, but the coat was dry. She called out but heard no answer.

Hello? she said again. Am I completely alone in here, even though the presence of another coat on the coat rack in the entryway seems to suggest otherwise?

There was no answer. There was no sound. There was very little light. She thought the bathroom was ahead, the first door on the left, and felt the need to go in and try the taps.

When she was a baby, her mother would hold her under the water tap. Hold her feet under flowing, warm water from the tap. It was a technique that she was taught by a midwife. The midwife said it was the best way to make a baby stop crying. It always worked.

The midwife said, A baby, when it cries, is usually attempting to make some sort of sense of the world. It is difficult to make sense of your own existence when you have had so little experience of it. A baby needs something that makes sense to happen. Flowing water makes sense. Babies understand, naturally understand, water running from a tap and over their feet.

Her mother had some trouble believing this. But the midwife was old and knew a lot about babies. She had had seven of her own children, and helped nine thousand and twenty mothers birth nine thousand, two hundred, and seventy-nine babies. She was a professional and her mother was merely an amateur. This was her first child. So the very first time the little baby girl cried, the mother took her to the bathroom, turned the cold and hot taps half open, unwrapped her baby's feet, and slowly placed them into the flowing water.

Here you go, she said. Here little Mary. This will help. Here little Mary. Here little angel of mine. Stop being confused. Consider the water running over your feet.

And she did. The little baby felt the warm water parting and flowing down either side of her foot. She felt it run down her foot to the bottom and spill off into the sink. Her little eyes, which could only see and comprehend a very little bit of visual information, managed to observe the water parting and then re-stitching itself back into one stream as it left her foot and fell to the basin. And spun down the drain. She felt the little film of water that stayed behind after it poured over her foot and into the drain. The behavior made perfect sense. The many consequences of water flowing over the baby's foot were inevitable, the baby thought. If this made sense, and made sense so quickly, it was clear that the things that were not making sense to her right now would probably make sense to her in their own time. The world would make sense. The world would reveal how reasonable it was, by and by. She took comfort in this.

Her mother fed her and took her to bed.

The woman found the bathroom in her uncle's house,

exactly where she thought it would be. She removed her sock and stuck her foot under the tap. She closed her eyes and opened the tap. She waited. She waited a little more. She did not feel comforted.

She felt a film of liquid on her foot. She felt it joining up at the bottom of her foot, and heard it dripping into the basin. But she did not hear it falling from the tap, and she did not feel it rushing over her foot. She did not feel the water being split into separate streams by her foot. She gave it a minute, but did not sense a change.

She opened her eyes and saw her blood pooling in the sink. The taps were dry. Nothing flowed out of them. Nothing had in a long time. The spout was cracked. The places in the basin not stained with blood were covered in dust. The bathroom was covered in dust. The light didn't work. She flipped the switch and nothing. Saw a broken mirror hanging from the bottom hinges of an empty medicine cabinet. The wood inside was brittle. It scraped off in splinters with barely a pass of her hand.

Her foot was still bleeding. She reached into her pocket and pulled out a leather case. In the case were glass bottles. In one of the bottles was a Skin Restoring beetle. She opened the bottle over her toe, and the little insect dropped out onto the raw, red digit. It began to vomit a peach-colored liquid, backing its way up in a spiral from the base of the skinless toe to the tip. When it covered the entire toe, it retraced its steps, exhaling hot, blue-tinted breath over the vomit, drying it, leaving a layer of something that appeared to be skin covering the injury. When it was done, she put the beetle back in his bottle, returned the bottle to the leather case, and returned the case to her pocket. Her toe felt much better.

Here we skim over a few minutes of time. She spent it considering a way to light her search through her uncle's house. There were long, long minutes of wondering and frustration. Said consideration ended when she realized, to her embarrassment, even though no one was around to help her accrete her feelings into full-blown shame, the curtains could be drawn back, and this would offer more than enough light for the coming hours—during which she could search for a circuit breaker panel allowing her to restore power to the entire, empty building.

We skipped that, though. Aren't you glad we skipped it? One imagines how frustrating it might be for a reader to participate in said consideration. One imagines how empathy might cause a reader to manifest feelings of their own deep embarrassment to have participated in said moments of missing the obvious. And consider, more, the fact that the act of reading makes this an act of willful ignorance, and that most readers would be doubly perturbed by finding out they are engaged in an act of willful ignorance. It is enough, one imagines, to turn one off the act of reading this narrative. And this narrative wants very much to keep its readers, not to cause them to hurl the book across the room—if only because this narrative does not want readers to unintentionally harm their drywall or break a mirror or send a precarious picture frame with, say, a beloved family photo toppling to the floor.

The house of her uncle was in a shabby condition. This was true even though her uncle had lived there until only very recently when it had been his good fortune to die there.

Shabby or not, it was a nice place for him to die. The house was filled with his things. He was familiar—as we all are, one suspects—with his things. With their shape. With their condition. With their age. With their scent. And his familiar things were the companions he had with him as he died. There were no family members at his side. No friends. No loyal companion animals. All he had were his books, his pictures, his lamps. An old lightbulb in a lamp by his bedside hummed as he passed away, and the sound followed him into the recesses of his brain, a drone melody of tiny, countering, cacophonous tones. He took a final deep breath through his nose, and the scent of his pillow cotton, ancient duck feathers, dried saliva and sweat, and the oils from his skin and hair—also walked beside him, a friendly little mist, as he turned the corners of the maze of his slowly deleting consciousness. A book slipped from his fingers, and that final experience of touch—the rough, leather cover rubbing down his fingers, and the weight of the spine and then the flat thumping of the full book on his groin—buzzed in the phantom body that he used to make the journey through the brain's badly lit corridors.

His brain was shabby, too. The wood needed to be stained again. The pictures and mirrors hung slightly crooked. A thin layer of dust, made mostly of his skin and no one else's because he rarely allowed visitors past his foyer, covered everything in the house and in his neural pathways. The couch in his brain was covered with an old sheet, too. The sink in his mind needed a good washing to scrub away the film of dried soap and toothpaste. The windows were so old in both places, they warped the images that passed through them. His world was skewed.

She had first been to her uncle's house when she was twelve. She had been, up to that point, unaware that she had an uncle. She had been, up to that point, unaware that she had a father, too, and that her father had had a brother. Or, better said, she was aware that at some point in the past she, like everyone else she had ever met, she had been ejected from someone's womb during the all-too-dramatic and painful process of labor and birth (the shouting, the body's fluids getting all over everything), and previous to that, she had been conceived of during the physical act of love between two people of the opposite sex (the shouting, the body's fluids getting all over everything), but one of the two people involved in those ceremonial events was not present in her life once that fluids had been wiped from her face and body. He had sat through the labor, sat through the delivery, and upon seeing her for the first time, realized that he had no idea what was supposed to happen next. So he improvised. He left. And he didn't return. And her mother never mentioned him. Let alone his brother.

But the uncle found his way into her life. He was like that. The uncle was expert at a few things, and one of them was inserting himself into people's lives regardless of their desire to see him so inserted. People can be like that if they are raised a certain way. It can be a useful, useful skill to those, say, who are ignored through much of their very early life. And the uncle was ignored quite vigorously through much of his early life.

And so he became an imposition. And so he found people with whom he wished to interact, and he wedged his way into the steady unfolding of their daily lives. They would be, one day, carrying on a very familiar conversation with a very old and very dear friend, and without warning, they would find they were responding to an aside offered by the woman's uncle. He was sitting at the dinner table with them as natural as can be. And they would, searching through the filecards of their memories, find that he had been to dinner with them before. Many times. They had invited him. When had they done that? When had he first appeared? They had no idea. They simply knew he was in with them for the long haul.

Remarkable.

At twelve, he had managed to find his way into her and her mother's life.

Little Anna, little Anna, little Anna, he'd say to her on the phone. What have you been up to today?

Little, uncle, she'd say.

It is good to talk to you, he'd say.

It is always good to talk, she'd say.

Your mother says you will visit, he said one day. You will visit for a week. I live up north. You will like it here. Maybe you will take the train?

I have never taken the train, she said. I have only taken cars.

You will adjust, he said. Trains have cars. It will, linguistically, be familiar.

And so she did. And then, there she was, her mother in tow, a bag in each hand, and there was the door to her uncle's house in the middle of a city up north. When the wind picked up, the coldest snow—so cold it would not melt into the thick carpet of snow on the roof—would blow off in clouds. It covered the two of them as they waited for their uncle to open the door and let them in. They were covered in a dusting of it. The doors pulled in and there he was.

He was tall and thin-shouldered. He was beaked and had almost no chin to speak of. His eyes were round and wet. His teeth were the largest teeth the little girl had ever seen.

Mirabella, he said. And you've brought your Mother. It's good to finally meet you.

He grabbed the bags from the two of them and carried them inside. He took coats and hats from them, pointed to nooks and racks for boots and gloves. He fed them warm potato soup with slices of bread and butter. He forced them to drink glasses of wine—a large one for the mother and a small one for the girl. And when her mother fell asleep in her chair, he gestured for the girl to follow him to the basement.

My brother was a terrible man to leave you, he said. A terrible man. I have not seen him for many years. But I want you to trust me. To know that I am with you. To know that I will conspire with you in any way I can. So I offer you this.

They walked through the basement, a collection of tall cardboard boxes, and jars full of nails and screws, and racks covered in balls of string and plastic toolboxes. They walked through the racks and past the boxes, and he led her to a little door.

I will now show you a crime, he said.

And you will know about it, he said. And you and I will be, for as long as we both live, in cahoots. You can choose to tell people about this. You can turn me in. I can go to prison. And then, our cahoots will not be. That is fine. If you choose to do so, I will accept that you have done so. But then I will not be around when you have a secret to hide and need a conspirator to assist you.

You are young and may not right now understand the value of having a conspirator. And you and I have just met, so you may not know why you should trust me when I say that one day, the value of a conspirator will be something that you will treasure. But I will ask you to consider my age and experience in matters like this.

She made no indication as to whether or not she was convinced. But it did not matter. He was going to open the door in the basement anyway and reveal to her his terrible crime. He was prepared for the consequences. And hopeful of the outcome.

The door opened to a room much larger inside than was possible. But she was still a little girl. Perspective was not her strong suit. It may have only seemed so. Inside the very large room, there were more than a dozen figures. People standing very still.

But not people. They were not made of flesh and bone and skin and hair. They did not breath and move and eat and sleep. They were made of something shiny and brown. They were brass. To the astonishment of the little girl, she found that she was in a room filled with statues. A monstrous crime. A terrible sin. Her uncle had purchased, or worse yet cast, a series of figures that represented people in three dimensions. To draw a person is fine. To photograph a person is fine. To film a person is a-ok. To take a pen and paper and describe a person in words? This is no crime. Why should it be? But to render a person in three dimensions, to represent a person—even an entirely made-up person—this is uncalled for.

They take up space! she shouted. They take up space as if they were just like real, living people!

Yes, he said. He smiled. Isn't it marvelous? Isn't it absolutely, positively marvelous to see them.

And she had to admit that there, in a room, with a

collection of statues, actual statues, that she could walk around, and look at from different angles, and touch—she had to admit that the experience was a little marvelous. Criminal, and wrong, and really very marvelous.

The circuit breaker panel was in the kitchen. The door had been papered over, but it was cut along its edges, and opened freely. The rows of switches were on, but the main was not, so she pulled it down, and heard the house whir just a little back to life. A fan above the stove began to spin. A light popped on. Light came in from the hallway. Light was seen down the hall. Light from up the stairs. Light under the door to the basement. She went down the steps to see if the room was still there.

The racks and boxes had been pushed around, had fallen in some places. Broken glass littered the floor, as did the odd screw and nail. Direct passage to the door in the back of the room was impossible without pushing some things out of the way, pulling others. It took time. But she made it, and found the door. It was unlocked.

It opened on the large room. It still, as an adult, appeared to her that the room was larger inside than it should have been. It was not just a trick played on her by her child's body, her child's eyes, her child's mind, her child's skewed sense of perspective. It had a high ceiling, much higher than in the rest of the basement, and much higher than was possible given the fact that it was under the floor of the house. A switch filled the room with light from overhead bulbs, which swung in a way that suggested wind was blowing above. The statues were still there. In fact, there were now two dozen. They were gathered together in a little crowd. She approached one and said hello.

How have you been? she said. It has been quite a while. I see there are some new tenants in the room, too. New roommates. Have they been here long? Have you spent time getting to know them? Are they quiet? Loud? She was speaking to the tallest. A male. Glasses. It stood with its mouth open but did not respond to her. It looked in her direction, and had a single finger held up on its right hand, preparing to answer her questions but never ever getting there.

Mr. February March, I presume, she said. And your wife, June July? How has she been?

She walked to a female statue near the male. The female was a nude. It held a hand in front of its face, a pose that might have either been shame at being caught in the nude, or the snickering pride of someone happy with her decision to appear nude before the viewer for erotic purposes. It was unclear.

She's an odd one, Mr. March, she said. But I wouldn't let her get away if I were you. This one is certainly a keeper.

She addressed each statue in its turn, walking from group to group within the crowd. They had been turned into couples and groupings of three. Conversations within a larger party.

I will miss you, she said. I will miss our little talks. I will miss these little talks. I will miss them. But I am going to burn you all up now.

And so she did. In a corner of the room, there was a great wooden barrel. On the barrel, there were four spigots. Below each spigot, there were long, branching trenches. The trenches webbed the floor. They disappeared under the walls. They went to every corner of the house. She turned the spigots, one by one. Liquid—strong-smelling, burning-in-the-nose, vaporous—flowed. Liquid followed the trenches. Liquid webbed the room. Liquid disappeared under the walls. She watched and she walked among the statues, and she patted them on the shoulders, patted them on the head.

Goodbye, goodbye, so long, goodbye, she said. See you probably never again, she said.

She was lying to them. She would never be able to see them again. She tried to, in her little way, comfort them with a tiny, tiny probably. But they appeared inconsolable. She failed and failed. The barrel emptied. She left the room and locked the door behind her. She went upstairs.

In the foyer, she opened the hall closet's door. It had swelled and she had to push down on the doorknob, push down and pull out to open the door. In the back of the closet, there was a small, square door with hinges on the top. She pulled it open and hooked a bent nail on looped screw into another looped screwed. From her pocket, she pulled a pack of matches she had picked up in the train's dining car. She opened the pack, pulled free a single match, lit it by closing it between the flap of the pack to the body of the pack and pulling it out across the striking surface. It popped. The small flame erupted as the match hissed at her. She lit the rest of the pack, and it erupted with a louder hiss. And she looked at it a moment. And she dropped it in the door. And it fell down a drop to a pool of the flammable liquid below.

She walked out the door and locked the door. She walked across the street and found a bench. She sat on the bench and waited to watch the building consumed in flames.

But it didn't happen.

SECTION V: ODESSA

A van approached and stopped in front of her. It's panel door opened and a man stepped out.

Hello, my dear, dear Odessa, he said.

Me? she said.

You, Odessa, he said. I am happy to see you. I am here for you.

I'm very busy right now, she said. I am waiting for my uncle's house to burn down.

Your uncle's house will not be burning down, he said.

I believe it will, she said. I did all the things I was instructed to do.

You did, I am sure Odessa. But the drop to the pool? It is filled with Grabber beetles. They have caught the, what, matches? She nodded. They have caught the matches and have carried them to some Blower beetles who have blown out the flames. The Grabber beetles will be along in a moment. Let's sit together and wait.

She said nothing. He sat down on the bench and pulled a pouch from his jacket. From the pouch, he fished out sunflower seeds, which he removed from his fingertips with the sticky end of his tongue.

I have quit smoking, he said. The seeds make my life bearable. What, Odessa, makes your life bearable?

Fire, she said. Only fire.

There will be none today, Odessa. There will be no conflagration. No destruction of this house. But don't worry. You haven't failed. You weren't really supposed to burn the house down to succeed in the first place.

Wasn't I? she said. It seemed to me I was.

Yes, well. There is another kind of success, and we are going to help you with that one instead.

A gentle wind whipped. Her nose ached at its tip. His leg shook as he sat beside her. He bounced it and bounced it. They did not speak until, from across the street, two beetles scuttled toward them. In the pincers of one, the half burned pack of matches. The other beetle followed close, and they fought over the pack. They grabbed and pulled. The bigger one kept hold. He bounced and he bounced.

Here they are now, the man said. Shall we get in the van and take a drive? He said, and stepped on the beetles.

I don't think so, she said.

Now, Odessa. We have a place to go. You, on your own, have no place to go. I, on my own, have a place to go. If you join me and make us a we, then we have a place to go. A nice place to go. A warm place to go. A place to go where things will happen. You like things when they happen. Everyone likes things when they happen.

Not all things, she said.

All things, he said. Everyone likes all things when they happen because when something happens, good or bad, it means that things are still moving forward. And even more things will happen. Every bad thing that happens is just the necessary preamble of the good thing that might happen next. It's an ingredient in the next things. If things don't happen, everything stops happening.

They can stop, she said. Why not we let them stop?

No, he said. Not today. They won't stop today. Let's go.

I can sit here and get covered in snow, she said.

He pulled an envelope from his overcoat. He opened it, and pulled a sheet of paper from it. The paper was yellow with a green filigree border. Certificate of Marriage, it said. Odessa Klam it said in the space for "bride." I have this, Odessa. We took it from your uncle's house a long time ago. Come with me now. Let's talk about this. Let's talk about your husband.

She rose and stepped into the van. He pointed to a seat, and she sat in it. And then from the darkness behind her, a fist appeared, a sap in its fingers descended on her skull, a cracking sound cracked, a shimmer of lights popped in her eyes, a hood covered her face, and all her thoughts stopped.

She woke to red light and nothing else. Close red light. She heard a rolling piano on a radio, static shushing with every downbeat of a drum played with brushes. She was on her back, her eyes open, and only red.

Turning her head, she felt the sheet above her. A red sheet diffused and colored the light in her eyes. Sleep beetles were sucking at her neck; she felt their gentle gnawings. Sleep beetles at her fingers. Sleep beetles at her toes. They were tired, themselves, slowing down. She was waking up. She pulled down the sheet and she was in a red bed with a red curtain around it. She sat up and saw her red pillow. She shook away the sleep beetles, and they fell. They wandered away, searching for their bottle. A red comforter. A man on the radio sang about red lips along with the rolling piano and the brushed drum beats. Deep red wooden posts. A man on the radio confessed to the listener that he loved her and very much loved her red, red lips.

She turned on her side and opened the curtain. A white room. An empty white room. A man in a white on white suit sat in a white wooden chair. He smiled a white-toothed smile. Your sleep has worn off, he said.

It has, she said. Where, please, am I?

Gosh, how should I know, he said.

Aren't you here as well, she asked.

I suppose that's true, he said. He stood and walked to the bed. May I get you a gown?

She was naked. She pulled the blood red sheet up over herself.

Oh, don't worry about that, my dear, he said. I've seen it all.

You're a doctor? she asked.

Oh, goodness, no, he said. Only that I've just seen it all in my time. A doctor, though. No. Never had the patience for that kind of study.

A gown would be nice, she said. He walked to a white dresser and pulled out a white gown. There were black circles at the shoulders of the gown. A trail of feathers down the back, where her spine would be.

This is a good one, he said. A very good one.

The room was very quiet. It was windowless. It was dry. It smelled a little like fresh paint. Fresh white paint.

You don't know where we are? she asked.

Not precisely, he said. We are at the base of a mountain, though. I've seen that through the window in my room.

Which mountain?

They all look the same to me, he said. This one appears big, though. A big mountain. We are at the base of a big, big mountain. We are guests at a home at the base of a big, big mountain. Lucky us.

Why are we here?

You were sleeping and I was watching you sleep.

Not the room, she said. I mean the home at the base of a big, big mountain. Why are we in a home at the base of a big, big mountain.

I am here to watch you sleep. Nothing more. I have been told that I will be allowed to go home after you wake up. And now you have woken up. I will be allowed to go home. To my family. I'm glad you did not sleep for a very long time. I love my family very much.

You were kidnapped? Like I was?

I suppose that's the word. He realized he was still holding her gown and handed it to her. Sorry about that. In his eyes, this very genuine apology. This very genuine appreciation.

It's all right, she said. She pulled the curtain back and put on the gown. You seem not so angry about having been kidnapped to watch a woman sleep.

What's the use in anger, he said. She pulled open the curtain again and slipped out of the bed. And, honestly, this happens far more often than you'd think. He smiled at her. In his mouth, this very genuine appreciation. He leaned in as if to embrace her. She leaned away.

Do you need to inform them that I am awake? she asked.

No, Odessa. I believe they already know.

My name is not Odessa, she said.

I honestly don't care, he said. I was told to watch Odessa, and they brought me here. As long as, even if your name is not Odessa, I am still given credit for having watched Odessa, I am happy.

His smile melted. You do think they will give me credit for having watched Odessa even if you are not Odessa, yes?

I really don't know, she said. I only know that I am not named Odessa.

If they ask, though, would you mind telling them that you are Odessa? I would really appreciate it. I really would like to get credit for this so I am allowed to go home.

I am not, she said, named Odessa. They want me to answer to that name, but I can't. I am not that person. I am not Odessa.

Oh, dear, he said. It's only that if you are not Odessa and I have been watching you, and I am supposed to watch an Odessa, this could mean I will not be able to go home. Perhaps it would be best if you were to answer to Odessa for my sake. Would that be all right? Would you do that for me? It's only that I love my family very much. His hands were slightly trembling. Remember when I got you the gown?

I'm very sorry, she said. I am not that person. I cannot let them make me that person.

But, don't you see, he said, yelling a little now, that I love my family and if I am not allowed to leave I will not be allowed to see them? He raised his hands to her. She stepped back. It's just that you must be who they want you to be if I am to be allowed to leave. You see that, don't you?

I, she said. His hands were on her. They were scrabbling and clawing to her neck as she fought him off.

It's very important, he said, yelling a little louder. It's very important to me and to my family, because of reasons of love, and the feelings of it that I have. This is why you must do this for me.

I, she said, but she had no excess air to push through her throat to speak anything more. He was obstructing it. He was bottling it up.

Love is a thing that we all enjoy, he yelled much louder.

We all enjoy it and need it and thrive on it, you see. I was watching you very, very carefully, and I was doing it because of the love inside me. Now you must help. Me. Out.

She struggled and saw red again. A brighter red, though. A fuller red than before. A red with flashing blue fireworks. A red sky with a green frame that pulled in and in and in. He was now just grunting. She heard little explosive sounds from him, and they sounded like a mangled version of the word "love."

But he fell.

His hands went limp and he fell to the ground. He went limp and fell forward and she stepped away and his back, she saw, was covered in beetles. They were nipping him. Dozens of them on his back, nipping and nipping. Blood appeared on his shirt, blood in the empty spaces where the beetles were not. Blood soaked through his shirt and to the white floor.

Beetles, she said.

It was a while before someone came to remove the body. What was left of the body. The beetles had had their way with much of it. She had gone back to the bed to lie down and wait, because it really seemed like there was no other choice. Nothing else to do. Nothing but wait.

The mountain slept quite soundly. No trees shook in wind. No mountain streams flowed meltwater from the top to the bottom. No dirt upturned or churned or even moved at the shouldering of bugs of claws of burrowing creatures. Just nothing at all happening. The mountain slept quite soundly.

The priests were happy to see the mountain in its doze. They circled together in a tall white room and held hands and smiled and clucked tongues at one another in a happy, happy way. Cluck and cluck and smile. That's how it was. You see? Many hours they sat and felt happy.

Odessa had come back to them. The wife had returned. They clucked happily at this, as well. The mountain, when it woke—and it was bound to wake again, eventually—would be pleased to see its bride back. And looking well. And looking the same as when she had left. His Odessa. The mountain's bride Odessa. What happiness.

What happiness was there. What happiness to be had, if only one looked for it.

Time passed. People got hungry. The cook was summoned. Requests were made. (Simple requests.) The cook took no notes. The cook walked to the kitchen. On the way, he stopped in to see Odessa.

Are you eating, he asked.

She did not answer.

Are you eating, he asked again.

She did not answer.

You should eat, he said.

She did not answer.

Can I make you something? Anything? Our kitchen is quite well appointed and our store rooms are quite well stocked. I am able to likely make whatever you want.

Odessa did not answer.

Food is very important, you know, he said. It is important in times of great stress especially—times like this time is for you—to eat and to keep eating and to do so whenever the opportunity presents itself. I have, over the years, known more than one person who has been in a kidnap-like situation, and I will tell you that to a person, they have all said to me, 'Brian, remember to eat if you are ever held somewhere and held in a way that seems like it is against your will.' They have all said to me, 'You know, Brian, I have got to tell you: I just wish I had eaten. I wish before I was taken, I had remembered to maybe have lunch, and I wish when I was there being held, I wish that when the folks who were holding me had offered me a sandwich or a granola bar or something, I wish I had said to them that yes I would like a granola bar.' So, really. I think you should eat, Odessa.

My name is not Odessa, she said.

The door says Odessa, he said. On a little slip of paper. It's not accurate?

It's not accurate, she said.

I will see if I can find someone who can help out with that, he said. I'll tell the priests when I go to see them with their food. Which, again, I would like to offer to you. You should have food. Have you had food? You should have food. I can bring food. What do you say, Odessa?

My name is not Odessa, she said.

The door still says Odessa. Until it has changed—which is a thing I will try to facilitate, Odessa, I promise—I will follow the words on the door. Will that be acceptable?

It will not, she said.

It is sad to hear that, Odessa. It is very sad to hear that.

It is sad to hear many things, Brian.

My name is not Brian, he said, and he walked out the door, and it locked behind him, and his footsteps clapped as he walked away and away and away.

Now is as good a time as any to make an accounting of your life, Odessa, said a man. I am going to sit here with this pad of paper and this pen and I am going to take notes. You say what you want to say, and I will record it.

The man had arrived with a tray of food. I'm not hungry, she said.

That's fine, said the man. I'll be more than happy to eat this, Odessa.

My name is not Odessa, she said.

I've heard that about you, said the man. I honestly do not care.

Then he said the thing about her making an accounting of her life. He had pulled a white chair up to the side of the bed.

She had gone back to lying in the red bed in the middle of the white room. She was wearing the gown, though it was not a proper garment for sleep. The feathers on the spine of the gown were molting onto the red sheets.

The man lifted the cover on the tray of food, grabbed a sandwich from the plate, and ate it. Sandwich in his left hand. Pen in his right hand. Pad of paper on his knee. He was ready for her to make an accounting. And he was eating the sandwich.

Begin somewhere, said the man.

But wherever I pick to being, she said, I do such a great disservice to every other possible beginning. It hardly seems right.

Nothing seems right, said the man.

Then maybe I should offer you nothing, she said.

Again, Odessa?

My name is not Odessa.

Then what is it? If it's not Odessa, what is your name? Maybe start there.

But my name is the beginning of nothing. My name does not set us off in any direction. If you want a story, and you want me to begin somewhere, you want me to find a beginning from which things will follow. My name does not do that.

No, said the man. That doesn't seem right. Lives begin with names. Stories begin with names.

Not mine, she said.

Your name is what, said the man, the end, then?

Not that, either. My name is not a stop on the journey at all. It is not the beginning, because I was not first given a name. My name is not a stop along the way of my life's journey, because it was not something I acquired at some point. It was not quested for. It was not a reward. It was not handed to me. It was not accidentally stuck to me one day. My name is not the top of a climb. My name is not the camp beside a lake where I will sleep and dream and die. My name is not a moment fondly remembered. It is not here or there or anywhere. It isn't.

Then we probably shouldn't begin there, said the man.

No, she said. But I don't know where else to begin.

Begin with Odessa.

I am not Odessa.

But you may as well be, said the man. Why not be? I don't know, she said. I just am not.

But it is better for us if you are. So you are, Odessa. Now, an accounting of Odessa's life. Begin.

SECTION VI: THE ACCOUNTING

She spoke:

The mountain lived at the nape of the queen's long and very elegant neck. The neck of a queen is long and elegant because it turns a queen's head so often, and always away from things. A neck that turns a head so often away from things is a neck with definition to its muscles. A neck with definition to its muscles is a neck that stretches long. A long elegant neck, like the neck of a queen, is one that is, over many years, made. It is worked for. It is the product of a queen's deliberate indifference to most of the things the world has to offer. The product of how often a queen turns her head away from things with her longer every day, more elegant every day neck. Remember this when you see a queen. Or when you live on the body of a queen. Remember this.

The mountain lived at the nape of the neck of the queen. The mountain lived at the lowest rung of the spine of the neck of the continent that was the queen. The mountain lived and waited. (Living is mostly waiting.) Slept and slept. (Living is mostly sleeping, or hoping soon to sleep.) Rumbled sometimes. (We rumble often.) Was quiet mostly. (We can't keep quiet or we can't keep still, most of us.) Shivered in winter. Dreamed of its wife. Expressed its dreams in the plants that it allowed to grow on its surface—it's rocky faces and its gentle, fertile slopes. Expressed its dreams in the way it directed the melting water from its icecaps to find corridors to the body of the queen, the rivers of the queen, the lakes of the queen. Expressed its dreams in the way that it allowed the clouds to halo its peak, allowed fog to obscure the whole of it from view. Expressed its dreams in the way it remained in place and did not roll over or tumble or break apart and settle flat on the ground.

The mountain lived at the nape of the neck of the queen, and thus knew only things about the neck of the queen. Not the hands and feet of the queen—which were, in fact, submerged in water. Not the thighs or elbows of the queen—where cities had not grown and people did not dare search for. Not the stomach of the queen or the pubic mound of the queen—where most of the people lived and worked. Not the head of the queen—where all the dreams of all the people all over the body of the queen came from. The mountain lived at the nape of the neck, alone.

Alone for a very long time. Until the day the mountain met his wife.

The wife of the mountain was heading north. She wanted to find the head of the queen. She wanted to find the place where her dreams came from. She wanted to enter the caves in the head of the queen and find, underground, the vast and clear pools where all the dreams formed. She had diving gear with her. She wanted to swim down through the clear water to the bottom, find the level where the water was not as clear, find the level below where it was hard to see. She wanted to rummage through the muck at the bottom of the pools of stuff—it's not water—that form the dreams of the people who live on the body of the queen. She wanted to rummage through and find the source material of her dreams. She wanted to take it from the muck, store it in her pack, return to her home, and throw it all in the fire. Burn it in the fire she used to heat her home.

The wife—then just a woman and not yet a wife—

told the mountain this story. The mountain fell in love. The mountain, too, had a weird and uncomfortable relationship with its dreams. It related to what the woman said, and it saw itself in the woman, and it wanted to make the woman its wife.

So the mountain trapped the woman. When the woman tried to cross over the mountain, she found that every time she reached what she thought was the summit, the mountain had a higher peak hidden in its cloud. When the woman tried to navigate around the mountain, the woman found that she would travel for a day, another day, another day, another day, and end up back where she had started. The mountain moved its landmarks, tricked her with trees that shifted when she looked away. The mountain made trails like möbius bands to send her around and back and forth and nowhere no matter how much she walked.

The woman did not starve. The mountain made food available to her. The woman did not give up. The mountain teased her with brief views of the head of the queen any time her spirit fell. The woman did not leave—and couldn't if she had wanted to. The mountain would've seen to that.

The woman remained on the mountain for years and years. Eventually, she spent so much time on the mountain that she, in the eyes of the state, became the wife of the mountain. They had been together so long, they were married in the eyes of the state. The mountain had married the woman. The woman had become the wife, benefiting from all the legal benefits and responsible for all the legal responsibilities that the marriage relationship hides within the boxes and drawers of its bureau.

But the wife had not wanted to be married to the mountain. She had wanted to journey to the head of the queen and spelunk in the head of the queen and dive in the clear pools hidden in the head of the queen and rummage in the muck deep in the pools in the head of the queen and find the stuff that made up her dreams that swam at the bottom of the pools in the head of the queen and take the stuff and return home and burn her dreams. That's what the wife wanted to do.

Instead, through trickery and patience on the part of the mountain, the wife had become the wife of the mountain. And the wife was angry.

The mountain was content. The mountain had its wife.

The wife was angry. How could she distract the mountain? How could she escape the mountain?

The mountain did not need meals, so no meal could be made to hide poison for the mountain. The mountain did not need sex, so no act could be devised to incapacitate the mountain with exhaustion or bliss or self-congratulations or self-doubt. The mountain needed nothing except the presence of the wife, it seemed.

The mountain, in trapping the wife, had been clever and resolved. In the keeping of the wife, the mountain was less attentive. The wife fashioned a wife in the rock face of a cliff of the mountain. She carved a wife into the mountain. She spent many hours on it. She spent many days on it. She fashioned a wife so perfect, it fooled the mountain. The mountain turned all its considerable attention to the rock-face wife. Its wife. And while the mountain stared at its rock-face wife—which was just a tiny piece of the mountain made to look like the real wife—the woman came down off the mountain. She separated from the mountain. She gave up on her journey to the head of the queen. She went home and lived her life.

Eventually the mountain noticed that the rock-face wife was not the real wife and it destroyed it. And it searched itself and could not find the real wife. And it lost hope and fell asleep.

She stopped speaking. The man closed his notepad, finished his sandwich, got up, and left.

Eat, Odessa, said the man.

My name is not Odessa.

May as well be, said the man. Really, though, who cares?

SECTION VII: THE MOUNTAIN

The mountain lived at the nape of the queen's long and elegant neck. The neck of a queen is long and elegant because it is turned often away from things. A neck that turns often away from things is a neck with definition to its muscles. A neck with definition to its muscles is a neck that stretches long. A long and elegant neck, like the neck of a queen, is one that is, over years, made. Worked for. It is the product of deliberate indifference. Remember this when you see a queen. Or when you live on the body of a queen. Remember this.

The mountain lived at the nape of the neck of the queen. The mountain lived at the lowest rung of the spine in the neck. The mountain lived and waited. Slept and slept. Rumbled sometimes. Was quiet mostly. Shivered in the winter. Dreamed of its wife. Expressed its dreams in the plants that it allowed space upon its surface—it's rocky faces and its gentle, fertile slopes. Expressed its dreams in the way it directed the melting water from its icecaps to find corridors to the body of the queen, the rivers of the queen, the lakes of the queen. Expressed its dreams in the way it allowed the clouds to halo its peak, allowed fog to obscure the whole of it from view. Expressed its dreams in the way it remained in place and did not roll over or tumble or break apart and settle flat on the ground.

The mountain lived at the nape of the neck of the queen, and thus knew only things about the neck of the queen. Not the hands and feet of the queen—which were, I will tell you, submerged in water. Not the thighs or elbows of the queen—where cities had not grown and people did not congregate. Nor did they search for the thighs and elbows of the queen. They did not map and locate. They did not wonder. Not after the thighs and elbows of a queen.

The mountain lived at the nape of the neck of a queen and that was all there was about that.

She was undressed. She was bound. She was washed. She was dressed. She was gagged. She was carried. She was placed in a circle of men. She was tisked. She was frowned upon. She was deliberately ignored. She was stared at. She was approached. She was pricked with needles. She was made to bleed.

Odessa, said a man. The man wore a hood. The men all wore hoods. Gray hoods, gray jumpsuits. No shoes, no socks. Feet painted gray. Wet paint that left ever-smaller tracks as they walked. Odessa, said the man, we're not so happy to see you.

She struggled a sound against the gag, but its articulation was rebuffed by heavy fabric. It limped out as a muffled vowel. An O.

Odessa, said the man, the mountain has missed you even as we have not. The mountain sleeps and sleeps and sleeps. Because it has waited for you to return. And here you are.

She struggled another sound against the gag, but again it was pushed mostly back into her throat. Another vowel. An A.

Tonight we might just wake the mountain, said the man.

Tonight with your help. Tonight with your participation, we may be able to wake the mountain.

She prepared to struggle another sound against the gag, but the man reached his hand out to her face and closed her eyes for her. He stroked her jaw. And stroked her jaw. And pulled her cheeks. And stroked her jaw. And there was pain. And there was a quick and flashing light. And she was under.

And awoke on a pedestal. Awoke prone. Awoke unbound, ungagged. Awoke no longer surrounded. Awoke at the foot of the mountain. Awoke to rain wetting her hair and clothes and face. Awoke.

And tried to stand. Her body would not obey. Her legs were numb, as were her arms. She could not shift. She could not roll. She could only, with great effort, move her neck. So she moved her neck. She turned to the mountain.

A distance away stood one of the hooded men. He had his back to her. His hands were raised above his head. He shook and shook. His body was substantial and then Insubstantial. He went in and out. His hands shook and shook. And he shook and shook. And he turned.

He pulled away his hood. His eyes were rolled back, white. Divorce, he said. The mountain gets his divorce, he said. Whether he wants it or not, he said.

A little saliva emerged from his mouth and it dribbled down his chin. And it hung a little rope off his chin. And it danced a little dance below his chin. And it broke and it fell. And in the dirt it splashed. And in the dirt it pooled. And in the dirt it grew.

The spittle puddle grew like hell. It grew and got so big, it spread out and burbled on its way to her on the pedestal. Her, on the pedestal. She, lying on the pedestal, unable to move.

The puddle alive and climbing the pedestal. The puddle alive and searching her out. The puddle alive and covering her feet, her legs, her pelvis. It climbing up her spine.

Stand, Odessa, said the man. And she stood. She felt pushed and pulled and moved by the film covering her lower body. It bent her at the waist. It turned her. It hopped her down from the pedestal. It stood her erect.

Walk, Odessa, said the man. And she walked toward the man. Toward the mountain. The other man appeared. The other men gathered around her in a circle.

Kneel, Odessa, said the man. And she kneeled in the center of a circle of men. In the shadow of the mountain.

Without the mountain, where would we be? said the man. But it sleeps because it pines for its wife. It pines for Odessa. And the pining often find it difficult to concentrate on all the other important things in life. The depressed often find it difficult to do anything other than sleep. Our poor mountain, depressed because his wife left him. Letting himself go. Just sleeping all the time. Wondering if it's all worth it. Having trouble with motivation. Angry at inappropriate times and inappropriate people. Gaining weight because it does not have the energy to be active and can't be bothered to eat healthfully. Our poor, sad mountain.

Amen, said the crowd.

Our poor, sad mountain, said the man. In a state of limbo since his wife left. Since she left and did not say where she was going. Our mountain, confused by his wife's behavior and unable to concentrate on anything. Left only to wonder about why she left and what he did to make her leave. Our poor mountain, so very confused by the way things have turned out in his life. Having tried so hard to make the relationship work, even though the participants in the relationship are so very different. And left alone and wondering by a wife who could not properly communicate her needs in a way that made sense to the mountain.

Amen, said the crowd.

Without the mountain, this is where we've been, said the man. Tired and cold and just as confused. And searching and searching. Looking for the wife, to bring the wife back to the mountain. So that she could explain to the mountain why she left. What emotional need he could not meet. Why it was really, in the end, not his fault. Nothing that the mountain did. That the two of them were just too different. That the relationship was doomed from the start. That they were from two different worlds.

Amen, said the crowd.

Our poor, sad mountain, said the man. Now the wife is here. But the wife can't explain a thing. The wife can't offer the comfort to the mountain that the mountain needs to move on with his life. She can only kneel here before it. Can't speak. Can't hold the mountain one last time. Can't even admit that she is the wife. We, all of us gathered here together, all of us friends of the mountain, have decided to do something for the mountains own good.

Amen, said the crowd.

Without the mountain, what's the point of us? said the man. So we do for him. And, sure, this isn't what he wants to hear. This might make the mountain angry with us for a short time. But we think that as things shake out, the mountain will grow to understand what we have done. The mountain will forgive us when he sees how much better off he is without the wife. This wife. This incomprehensible wife. This wife who will not meet the mountain half way. This wife is not the wife for the mountain. This wife is nice and all, but not well-suited for the mountain.

Amen, said the crowd.

Our poor, sad mountain, said the men. We're just trying to help.

Amen, said the crowd.

This is divorce, said the man, pulling a pistol from his robe.

Amen, said the crowd.

We divorce you from the mountain, said the man.

Amen, said the crowd.

We hope you get where we are coming from, said the man.

Amen, said the crowd.

And the man shot Odessa.

And again, she was out.

Observe it. This land was built on the body of a queen. Over the trestles built upon her gown, a train was making its way North. The destination sat in the sternum, in the cold, hard center of her. It was winter.

ACKNOWLEDGMENTS

I acknowledge you.

Matthew Simmons lives in Seattle. He is the author of a novella, two story collections, half a novel, and 11,000 tweets. More at matthewjsimmons.com and @matthewjsimmons.

OFFICIAL

CCM ●

GET OUT OF JAIL
✳ VOUCHER ✳

- - - - - - - - - - - - - - - - - - - -

Tear this out.
Skip that social event.
It's okay.
You don't have to go if you don't want to. Pick up
the book you just bought. Open to the first page.
You'll thank us by the third paragraph.

If friends ask why you were a no-show, show them
this voucher.
You'll be fine.

- - - - - - - - - - - - - - - - - - - -

We're coping.

●

Made in the USA
Middletown, DE
27 January 2017